SHOW QUEEN

RENÉE DAHLIA

SHOW QUEEN
RENÉE DAHLIA

They're real life enemies, but online they're besties. . .

Stubborn disabled dance club owner meets demisexual property tycoon in this ff enemies to lovers romance.

Seraph's Burlesque Club owner Beth Zendeli takes no nonsense. She hustled to keep her club afloat through lean years and a pandemic, and she doesn't let her disability define her. But her perfect location has been sold, and the club is being evicted.

The new owner is unreasonable, immovable, and irritating. In desperation, she turns to the online friends she talks about plants with. . .

Property investor Liz Whitten has plans for the old building she's just purchased, and she's used to getting her way. But when she meets the leaseholder in real life, a chance statement reveals Beth to be Liz's online friend QueenB.

Can she really evict a friend? Especially a friend who is so unexpected and fascinating in real life.

Liz must decide if profits and ideals matter more than friendship, or if it's worth taking a risk on love.

Tropes:
Enemies to lovers
Seasoned romance (older main characters)
Online friends to IRL lovers
Friends online and enemies IRL

ABOUT THE AUTHOR

Renée Dahlia is an unabashed romance reader who loves feisty women and strong, clever men. Her books reflect this, with a side note of awkward humour. Renée has a science degree in physics. When not distracted by the characters fighting for attention in her brain, she works in the horse-racing industry doing data analysis and writing magazine articles. When she isn't reading or writing, Renée spends her time with her partner and four children, usually watching them play cricket.

For all my online friends who made the pandemic bearable.
You are all wonderful.

FOREWORD

Welcome to SHOW QUEEN, the final book in the Seraph's Burlesque Club series.

This series consists of three lesbian romances is set in a burlesque club in London. If you love to read about a found family with queer people who thrive, this series has that and more.

If you love online friends but enemies in real life, and older main characters who think they already know what they want in life, then you'll enjoy this one.

Please note this series is set after the COVID pandemic and assumes everyone is vaccinated. It's a bit of a post-pandemic fantasy that doesn't really reflect reality, unfortunately. There is also a car crash death (not on page) and one character who became an amputee in the same crash. There is discussion around the death of a parent.

This book is written in Australian English and some of the spelling and phrases may be unfamiliar to American readers.

If you are keen to keep up to date on new releases and,

more importantly, sales, I recommend you sign up to my newsletter at http://www.reneedahlia.com or follow me on social media

Twitter
https://twitter.com/dekabat
Facebook
https://www.facebook.com/reneedahliawriter/
Instagram
https://www.instagram.com/reneedahlia_author/

I hope you enjoy reading this book!
Renée

1

AUTUMN

"Turn, extend your right leg to the front, bend, slide your hands up your leg as you stand again, then flick your hair." Beth ran through the dance step in slow motion as she talked, then watched everyone in her beginner's class copy her. Most people who attended dancing lessons at Seraph's Burlesque Club in London came for fitness and to gain some body confidence. Only a few ended up dancing on the stage here in the evenings. Beth adored all her dancers, and she loved teaching the art of burlesque. It was so good to be back to in-person classes.

"Yes, that's it. Amy, a little straighter with your leg. Sneha, great balance, and Kate, lovely big stride there. It really emphasises your leg length. Shall we do it again?"

Everyone looked great. "Excellent work. Now we are going to add an arch and twirl. Like this." Beth talked it through as she demonstrated. "First, step forward with your left leg so both feet are aligned and hold the stance with your legs a little wider than your shoulders, then bend over. Make it hot! Keep your arse sticking out and your spine with a slight arch in it. That's why we call it an arch! A little tip is to keep your head level with your hips, then rise up slowly back to a stance. Remember burlesque is all about the tease, so don't be subtle. Be seductive. Once you are upright again, twirl those hips. Understood?"

The class of beginners nodded. "Okay, let's go." She smiled as she repeated the movement for everyone. The energy in this room as they all copied her was her favourite part of this job. "That's a great start. Everyone practise a few more times and I'll come around the room and help each of you." She walked around, correcting the dancers' positions, as everyone tried the move.

"That's great, everyone. Let's put it all together, and that'll do for today. Ready?"

"Yes." The enthusiastic response made her grin. Running her own burlesque club was her life's passion, and finally being able to open up and hold dance classes again was such a thrill. Everyone who attended a class at Seraph's Burlesque Club had to be fully vaccinated against the cursed COVID that'd nearly destroyed her business and killed far too many people.

She walked back to the front of the class. "Okay. Let's put it together with the music." She flicked the remote that she had tucked in her pocket and music filled the studio. Dance classes, and the energy of the people who attended, made up for the ongoing worry about the future of the club. Almost. Several weeks ago, she'd learned that the building rented by Seraph's had been sold to fuck knows who and since then, she'd spent too many nights awake stressing about what might happen now. Likely nothing would change since she hadn't heard from the real estate company who managed the property. Back when her building had first been listed for sale, she'd done the sums and confirmed her suspicions. She definitely couldn't afford to buy it. Commercial real estate in London was so far out of her range that it wasn't even worth attempting to dream about buying it. It hadn't stopped her staring at the numbers and laughing with despair.

"Excellent work everyone." She turned off the music again. "If you feel ready, add your hands to the arch movement by stroking them down your thighs as you bend down and up as you rise." She showed them what she meant and a few people in the class made an oh sound as they understood how it all worked together. She loved it when a dance just clicked for someone. "Okay, let's go. From the top."

After the dance class, she had an hour to head upstairs to her flat and eat a very late lunch before she needed to prepare the club for tonight. Her stump ached as she climbed the stairs; it always did after a dance class, but she wasn't going to give up teaching anytime soon. After she'd lost her leg just below her knee in a car accident, she'd given up performing as a burlesque dancer. She'd invested the insurance payout in her own club and now she watched other dancers perform on her stage. The classes were hell on her stump, but she managed with a decent prosthetic and besides, demonstrating for her students helped keep her fit and connected to dancing. These stairs were the only shitty thing about Seraph's. There were many things she loved about this old building; the location and being able to live at her place of business were her favourites. The lack of a lift was not one of them.

By the time she'd come inside her flat and made a coffee,

she was happy to collapse in front of her computer. Before she opened her email, she logged into the Plant Parent group. It was her guilty pleasure. The group had grown exponentially during the lockdowns as people brought the outdoors inside, and as a long term member she'd signed up to be one of the admins. Maybe someone in the group would decide today was a good day to start a feisty argument over the best way to grow succulents in dim light, or something. Anything to distract her from her problems. The heady days of the 'most diva plant' were a distant memory. Obviously it was a maiden hair fern; she'd never been able to keep those alive. Perhaps she could start a new thread to keep everyone occupied and entertained. It'd certainly be more fun than worrying. It wasn't like she had any control over what happened with the building now anyway. Life had taught her to try not to worry about the future. Bad things happened and she could deal with them when they did; or at least, that was the theory. Her brain didn't always cooperate. Beth gulped down the rest of her coffee and checked her DMs.

NotTheQueen: Can you believe how much everyone is losing their minds over Monty Don's planned visit?

Fucking hell, she'd forgotten about that. She chuckled at her friend's comment, then read through some of the group. It'd been a coup to get the famous gardener to join the group for an online chat and many people were really excited. Whoa, a bit too excited in one case. She shared the comment to NotTheQueen.

QueenB: Who knew his hands would cause such a flutter? :D

She didn't expect an answer right away. NotTheQueen

wasn't often online at the same time as her anymore. She reached up to stretch her shoulders before she cooled down too much after the class.

NotTheQueen had been a much needed social contact during the long lockdowns. It'd never mattered that they didn't know each other's real names, they were too busy talking about other stuff. They used to chat in the evenings when Beth couldn't open Seraph's and she had nothing better to do, but now everyone was vaccinated and life had returned to, well, it wasn't normal or the same as before… There wasn't really a word for how life was now compared to before the pandemic. Occasionally, Beth wondered if they should meet up in real life, but she wasn't sure she wanted to change their friendship like that.

NotTheQueen: Yeah. I don't get it. They look like normal man hands to me.

QueenB: Ha! Must be a straight thing?

NotTheQueen: Maybe it's about competence. He gardens with his hands, and he's good at it, so…

QueenB: Must be.

NotTheQueen: Admin during the session is going to be a pain. Will you be around for it?

Beth opened her email to check her calendar, even though she knew she'd be downstairs working at Seraph's given that the online chat with Monty Don was scheduled for 8pm on a Friday night. She could probably log in from the back room to avoid an extra trip up the stairs. If she missed an hour or two, her bar manager Steph would easily be able to cope. Beth employed a great collection of people and they'd easily be able to run Seraph's without her involvement if needed. The issue was that Beth didn't like to be away from her club, her baby, for too long. It probably made her a pain in the arse of a boss, always hovering around everyone, but too bad. The club was hers. It was her financial wellbeing on the line every night, and more than that, she just bloody loved it there.

QueenB: Yeah, I'll be there.

NotTheQueen: Awesome. Let's have a drink and watch the shenanigans.

There was a new email in her inbox from an address she didn't know. She read it quickly. No. Fucking no. An eviction notice. The new owner hadn't wasted any time in throwing her out. Fucking hell. So much for trying not to stress about worst case scenarios. They'd just become incredibly real.

Beth ignored NotTheQueen's message and leaned back in her chair with her eyes shut. What now? She needed a plan. She really didn't need the added stress of an eviction notice… Right after they'd spent all that lovely COVID grant money on a renovation. There had to be something she could do… She drummed her fingers on the desk for a while, staring past her computer screen at the miniature weeping fig that sat on the far corner of the desk. What to do? She picked up her coffee for another sip only to discover she'd already drunk it all. Eventually, inspiration filtered through the panic, and she picked up her phone and called her IT specialist.

"Ben. How good are you at cyber stalking?"

"Good afternoon Beth."

"Answer the question." Beth heard her tone and breathed in and out a few times. There was no need to take out her stress on her highly competent employee. "I'm sorry. Good afternoon."

"Tell me the problem." To his credit, he ignored her nonsense.

"Right. You know how the building was sold recently?"

"Yeah?"

"Um, I want to talk to the new owner without lawyers. Is it possible to find out who bought the building?"

"What's going on?"

Each of her team at Seraph's were her family, and family stuck by each other. She whispered the truth. "They want to end our lease."

"And you want to talk to the new owner without lawyers getting in the way, and convince them otherwise?"

"Yes."

"It's a good plan. Seraph's is a booming business. I'll see what I can find out."

Beth's hands trembled a little. "Thanks. I just hope the new owner isn't some bigot, because—"

"—then we are all screwed." Ben understood. Seraph's wasn't just a club, it was a safe space for everyone who worked there. "It'll be okay. We'll find a new place."

Beth wished she had the same optimism. Space in London was always at a premium, even after so many businesses had gone under during the lockdowns. She'd been so lucky to find this building. It was close to a tube station and on a busy road with lots of foot traffic and had zoning to allow her to stay open until after midnight most nights of the week.

"Thanks Ben. I appreciate it." She ended the call and deliberately clicked away from her emails.

NotTheQueen: For Monty Don, we'll have to drink Full Monty's – vodka and Galliano over ice with grated ginger. You keen?

QueenB: That does sound good. How long until Friday?

NotTheQueen: Why? You want to start now? :D

QueenB: It's been a shit day

NotTheQueen: Oh no. What happened?

QueenB: Landlady issued an eviction notice

NotTheQueen: Crap. Do you need some financial help? I can send you some names of people to talk to.

QueenB: Thanks. No, it's not about money. Building has a new owner, so it's out of my hands

NotTheQueen: Blast. It happens though.

QueenB: Yeah. Still sucks.

NotTheQueen: It does.

QueenB: Yeah

If Beth had anything to do with it, she wouldn't be moving. Perhaps it was a little wild, but she wanted to hunt down the new owner and convince them to let her stay. She was a good tenant.

Beth logged out before she was tempted to re-read that damned email again. Nothing good would come from stressing about it, and she needed to get downstairs and set up the kitchen for tonight.

2

Liz didn't appreciate the little twinge of guilt at her friend's comment about her landlady. It meant nothing that she'd used landlady not landlord; Beth often switched out gendered words away from the masculine, using either feminine or neutral terms instead, just to make the point to people. It was just timing; plenty of buildings were bought and sold every day and owners often requested their tenants move after a sale had gone through. She ought to know, she'd just had her lawyers send out a similar request to the business occupying her latest purchase. Her fiftieth property, a number which shouldn't matter in a nearly thirty-year career investing in property, but in a couple of months, she'd be fifty and the coincidence seemed designed to remind her of her age.

She was proud of herself, proud that she'd made it this far through life on her own skills. There'd been a few setbacks along the way, and yet, here she was. Successful and thriving.

Most likely QueenB referred to her residential place of

rent, and besides, they were online friends, QueenB could be anywhere in the world. With that justification, Liz pushed away the niggling coincidence.

NotTheQueen: If you need any help, just reach out

She didn't expect to get an answer. It was just one of those things that people said to send comfort to friends, and QueenB was her friend. Not one of her closest friends—like Gita or Sreesha—just someone she could happily spend an hour or two with sharing memes and gifs as they both volunteered as admins on the Plant Parent group. When she'd first agreed to help out, she'd had no clue that people could get so uptight and argumentative over their opinions on indoor plants.

She really ought to visit her new building and start thinking about talking to an architect about the planning process. During the pandemic, she'd become accustomed to working remotely and didn't need to visit a site to do her due diligence. She had all the resources of the internet and several trusted advisors, who'd proved their worth a long time ago. But she missed doing that part of the process. She should check out the pub that was in her building. Maybe they would have a lunch service. She opened up the file from her lawyer, and then googled the business. Seraph's Burlesque Club. Huh. Not what she was expecting; she'd figured it was some chain owned pub leased to a franchise holder that had managed to stay open thanks only to the franchisee's backing. She really ought to have known this before she bought the building, but then, buildings like this hardly ever came up for sale and she'd jumped in quickly to beat the competition for the outstanding location. Only the size of the land and the street mattered, the rest were pesky details that would be dealt with after she owned it.

The website mentioned they were holding a Drag Trivia event tomorrow night. It sounded fun and gave her time to plan the outing. She could invite some friends along. Sreesha was a gun at trivia, and he'd coax several other ramblers along too. Liz bought a free ticket using their online store and was pleased when it arrived in her inbox immediately.

L iz stepped out of her ride share car and stood across the street from her latest purchase. It was exactly as her advisors had said; a solid boring brick building, quite obviously a converted 1940s factory with no real redeeming features. It would be no loss to London's architectural history to knock it down and replace it with a modern apartment building, something that had green credentials. Liz loved the trend for high rise living to include vertical gardens and she could imagine a new building bringing much needed greenery to this urban environment. If she could buy the rundown shops next door too, she'd be able to create something quite special. The real estate agent hadn't mentioned them. She really ought to get back into the habit of visiting all her potential investment sites before making a final decision.

Liz: I'm here. How far away are you guys?

Gita: Traffic sucks. Still about 20. Grab a table and a drink

Liz: Ok

Gita: Are Matias and Sreesha coming? We haven't done trivia in ages.

Liz: Yeah, they are. It should be fun.

It'd been forever since she'd caught up with her hiking group. Matias and Sreesha had been the ones to introduce her to rambling; a very British term for hiking over farmlands and tramping through woods on long walks. She'd met them over twenty years ago—*had it really been that long?*—when she bought the property that housed Sreesha's family restaurant, and during their first hike together, she'd met her best friend Gita. Gita had met her partner Harlan a few years later. Twenty-three years; holy hell. What was with the constant reminders that her fiftieth was around the corner? If she told her friends, they'd definitely want to throw her a party. Maybe she should mention it. With a smile on her face, she crossed the road and walked up the steps to the front door. She pulled out her free online ticket to show the huge security guy.

"You don't really need those tonight. Trivia is usually our quietest night."

"But your website said they were compulsory."

He nodded. "Yes, it's from when we first opened after the lockdowns and we needed to have a cap on numbers as well as ensure only vaccinated people booked."

"Oh. You should keep that. It made me feel safe in coming here." Liz never used to be anxious about going out in public. She'd always been sociable… before.

"Thank you. Creating a safe place is the focus of Seraph's Burlesque Club." The security guy grinned and waved her through the door. "Please come in."

Liz was struck with an unusual emotion, almost as if it

would be a shame to knock down such an inviting, safe, place. Since when did she ever blend emotions with her property work? Some properties were worthy of renovation and restoration. Others were like this one: bland, boring, and the whole neighbourhood would be improved by having a vibrant new building there. Stepping inside was like walking into a 1920s speakeasy, except a modern version of the same. The lighting drew her eye to the bar and the stunning red haired woman working behind it. Her smile welcomed Liz into the space.

"Hello. What can I get you?"

At the end of the bar was a display of indoor plants, a sago palm in an old oak barrel surrounded by several smaller pots filled with spider plants that spilled nicely, and a heart philodendron in a striking black pot. They reminded her of this morning's conversation with QueenB about the Monty Don event at the end of the week and she couldn't help herself.

"I'll have a Full Monty, thanks." The joke was lost on the bartender. Would it be weird to take a selfie with the drink once it was made and upload it to the Plant Parent group? Probably. Like most people in the group, she used a photo of her own garden as an avatar.

"Coming right up. Are you here for the trivia?"

"Yes."

"Brilliant. Our Reiko always has the best questions. You'll love it." The bartender was very enthusiastic. Her hands flashed as she grated ginger into the cocktail shaker, then poured in Galliano and Vodka. The whole thing was a masterclass in competence and that pesky guilt nudged her again. She probably shouldn't have come here because she was starting to doubt her plans. That never happened.

"Here you go." The bartender slid her glass over the shiny wooden bar and placed the EFTPOS machine beside it. Liz tapped to pay.

"Thanks."

"Anytime. Just grab any table you want. Helen Back will be here soon to get things started."

"Hell and Back?"

"Helen, last name Back, she's the queen who runs trivia. And definitely not to be confused with one of our former dancers of the same name."

"It's a clever name." Liz wondered at the story behind the bartender's vehement words, but not enough to ask her about it.

The bartender grinned. "Tell her that and she'll give you extra points. And hey, you didn't hear that from me." She winked and Liz smiled back at her. In the time she'd ordered her drink, several of the tables had started to fill up and now a collection of people lined up along the bar. Another woman, older with short black hair, clipped on one side close to her skull, joined the bartender and started taking orders. Liz walked towards an empty table and put her drink down. She checked her phone. No updates from her friends yet, so she scanned her emails and then flicked through her social media. She laid her phone on the table and sipped her drink, slowly taking in the room, unable to stop thinking about it from an investment point of view. The room had a simplicity, as if designed for people to enjoy themselves without the distraction of their surroundings. All the little details were carefully thought out, even down to the tables themselves. Hers had an incredible painting of a landscape; quintessentially English with the Cerne Abbas Giant chalk figure and his huge penis drawn against the hillside. Was she really thinking about knocking this place down? The people at the table next to her laughed loudly. Could she really destroy happiness? It wasn't like her to feel this... What was it? Sentimentality? She downed her drink and went back to the bar to grab another one.

3

Beth cast her gaze across the room. She had the latest menus in her fist, and really should distribute them to all the tables of people sitting there for trivia. It was one part of Seraph's that she couldn't seem to get consistency with; and tonight she was going to babysit another new kitchen hand. The club had a basic commercial kitchen and didn't do much more than bar nibbles because their clientele didn't come here to eat. If it wasn't for the threat of eviction hanging over her, she'd think—again—about hiring a decent chef and adding a dinner service to Seraph's.

"Beth. How's the new cook?" Reiko approached her.

"Hasn't arrived yet. Hopefully he's better than the last one. He was spectacularly useless." Beth didn't think it should be that hard to find someone to deep fry snacks. Finding reliable workers was a problem that plagued the hospitality industry. She was grateful for the staff she did have; Steph, Walter, Reiko, and Charlie. Especially Charlie, who ran all the shows and found new talent for the burlesque stage. Beth used to love doing that, but running the business took too much of her time and she'd needed to hand over that task to someone else. She'd been at risk of burnout when she'd employed Charlie, and Charlie had the added advantage of being able to dance and MC the show too. Beth's time on stage had been over many years ago. This was her joy now, creating the atmosphere where other dancers could thrive and where customers would be comfortable returning over and over to enjoy the show.

"I'll take those and hand them out if you want."

"Thanks. It looks like a few new people tonight."

Reiko scanned the room. "Yeah. That group over by the left are new. Most of the others have been here a few times before."

"It's good to see the crew together too." One table was surrounded by several of their regular dancers; Yolande, Jack, Dan, Charlie, and their costume designer, Ace.

Reiko smiled. "You've got a great business model here. All your dancers come back on other days to spend the money they've earned."

Beth knew that Reiko was joking, but it just didn't satisfy her the same way it would have. "I'd join them, but I have to coach the new cook in the kitchen tonight."

"It'll be fine. Or at least, I'd be willing to bet it won't be as bad as that bloke who lasted less than an hour before he cut his thumb and needed stitches."

"Oh God. Don't remind me. Seth? Was that his name? Why is it so hard to get kitchen staff?" Beth knew why and the solution was one she needed to put a lot more thought into. It was hard to get a kitchen hand who could cook a few bar snacks. No real chef wanted the gig because it was a waste of their talents, and the people who did apply were those with little ambition who just needed steady income. As soon as they got a better offer, they left. Tonight's menu was simple; cheese and crackers on platters for each table, or a dessert version with fruit and nicely arranged brandy snaps from a packet. Steph and Reiko had the bar sorted, so she went back into the kitchen to prepare. Jonti should be here in a few minutes, otherwise she'd be running the kitchen herself. Again. If there was any reason to get rid of the threat of eviction, it was this. She needed to employ a proper chef and get a decent dinner service happening. Even if the food only broke even, it didn't matter, it would attract more customers and give an improved service. She sighed; all her plans were in jeopardy now. She had much bigger problems —like finding a new place to lease—than solving the kitchen hand issue. She probably shouldn't even bother to dream or make plans until she knew what was happening.

B eth collapsed on her bed at the end of a long night, then removed her leg, stashing it in its usual spot. The new cook, Jonti, was an incredible find, and she wished she could offer the Black American chef something more than running her pathetic kitchen service. He'd recently moved to London and was grateful for the work. Her brain ran with possibilities and there was only one thing that ever helped quiet her down. She used her cane to cross her apartment, quickly showered and towelled herself dry, before diving under the covers of her bed. Autumn was in full swing and the nights were cold now. She grabbed some massage oil and rubbed it into her stump. The usual pain rushed up her thigh as she went through the motions of keeping herself healthy. Maintenance first, and then pleasure later, because her brain was still spinning.

Okay, time to deal with the mess in her brain. It'd become routine; grab the vibrator and slide it over her nipples first, then lower across her stomach, and then against her labia. She had a system and it never failed her. As she pushed the vibrator hard against her clit, the noise in her head started to fade. Sure, it would be temporary, but right now even the shortest reprieve from the catastrophes taking up all her energy would be worth it. Even after her accident, she'd always had faith in her body. Losing her leg below her knee had been a big change but she'd adjusted. Just as she would adjust again. She was bloody proud of herself. *Oh, yeah.* Heat spread across her skin, gooseflesh rising, and she said it again.

"I'm proud of myself. I'm a survivor." With her other hand, she pumped three fingers inside her, stroking herself while holding the vibrator against her clit and she came. Bliss. Beth let the endorphins take over and slowly sank into the mattress with her eyes closed. She turned off the vibrator and put it on the floor beside her bed. Tomorrow, she'd clean it, but right now, she let her body fall into the relief of her orgasm and into sleep.

～

Beth's phone rang and she groaned. She twisted in bed to grab it. "Ben." Hopefully her IT guy had some information on the new landlady.

"Good morning, Beth." He sounded way too chirpy and happy for a new day. What time was it anyway? In the background she heard Dan murmur something and she let herself smile. Dan had danced for her for years, but only recently had fallen in love with Ben during a trip together to the Greek Islands. They were both being cagey about it which meant there were probably juicy details she should ask them about sometime.

"Yeah." She pulled her phone from her ear to check the time. Ten in the morning. Okay, she'd had a normal amount of sleep. Why did she feel like she'd been run over by a freight train?

"I have good news."

"Give it to me." Please. Anything to get her into a positive headspace.

"The new owner is a Ms Liz Whitten. She's available to meet you on Friday at five in the evening for ten minutes."

"Ten minutes. Is she for real?" Beth wasn't going to be brushed off so easily. Who did this Ms Whitten think she was?

"Yes. It's better than nothing, so I've accepted the meeting for you. I'll text you the address." Ben was right. Beth was hardly in a position to negotiate for more time, although it hardly boded well for a decent resolution.

"Thanks Ben. I guess I have a couple of days to finalise what I want to say."

"I'm here if you need anything. I could make up a portfolio with some photos if you think that will help."

Beth breathed in. "Everything will help. We already have the grant documents from the refurbishment, so start there. Thanks."

"Will do. I just wanted to say that this job has been brilliant for me. You hired me when I was in a rough patch, and it's been amazing. Of course I'll help you. We all want to save Seraph's." She'd met Ben in the Plant Parent group, and when she'd heard he'd been sacked by his previous employer, she'd hired him as the stage technician and IT person for the club. Ben was brilliant, something Dan must have recognised too.

Beth tried not to think too hard about how everyone in her little Seraph family had a partner, while she had her hand and her vibrator. She shook off the loneliness; six weeks ago had been the thirteenth anniversary of her car crash. The one that had killed the love of her life, Jewel, and left her disabled. Navigating this time of year was always tricky. Jewel. She'd fallen in love so naturally when she'd been young. Jewel had swept her off her feet completely and when Jewel had died, it'd torn Beth's heart out. Grief was a bitch.

"Friday. I have to admin the Monty Don thing. Shit."

Ben laughed. "It's fine. I made sure the meeting was in a café close enough to here that you'd make it back by seven for admin duties. I don't envy you; Grandma is so excited. Every day this week, she asks me if it's Friday yet."

"It's going to be fun. And I'll definitely need it after meeting our new landlady. Fuck."

"It'll be fine. This Liz character will meet you and hear how cool Seraph's is and we'll all be fine."

"Yeah, I'm sure I'll woo her with my ultra coolness." Beth scoffed. At forty-two, she was too old to be considered cool.

"I mean it. We are going to make a kick arse presentation and you will wow her."

If only she had the same faith in people as Ben did.

There was a Finnish saying that she'd once heard a sports person say on the news. "The dogs are barking but the train keeps going." If a pandemic couldn't stop Seraph's, then a new landlady wasn't going to end the business either. Let the new owner bark as loud as she wanted. Beth wasn't giving up the fight anytime soon. Ben was right, she needed her club to survive, for her employees, and for herself.

"We will. I'll see you tonight, and make sure you log any overtime that you spend on the presentation."

"Okay. I'll text you the meeting stuff now."

"Thanks." It was time to focus on strategy for this meeting. A combative approach—fighting for her club—probably wasn't the best way forward. She needed to know what motivated her new landlady and how to convince her to let her stay. Before she headed downstairs to work, she'd sit down at her computer and research the heck out of Ms Liz Whitten, then she'd make her fall in love with Seraph's Burlesque Club.

Corporate seduction; if that was a thing.

4

———

Agreeing to this meeting was out of character, and Liz knew it. She liked to keep distance between herself and her tenants, and her lawyers had advised against it too. But after the hilarious evening at the club doing Drag Trivia with the delightful Helen Back, she'd let temptation rule over good sense. Sreesha had shown why he was the trivia champion and they'd won a bar tab that'd made the night even better. All of that added up to why she was sitting here in a local café, against her better judgement, drinking a freshly squeezed orange and ginger juice, waiting for the owner of Seraph's Burlesque Club to arrive for a meeting. She knew what would happen. The owner would try—and fail—to convince her to keep the lease in place. And Liz would feel even worse for giving them this tiny piece of hope before she took it away again. Why was she doing this to herself? It was a shame to have to move them on. Plans were plans though, and the club would find another location. Perhaps if she helped the club owner find a new lease, it might alleviate her guilt over kicking them out and maybe something good would come from this meeting after all. Gah. She should just leave before this mess got worse.

The door to the café opened and the woman from behind the bar walked in. The one with the short black hair, slightly longer over her fringe. Did they call that a pixie cut? Liz didn't know; she kept her own boring straight brunette hair pulled back in a practical bun. The woman wore a brown leather jacket over a light blue lacy top, and her jeans clung to slender thighs. If it wasn't for the slight limp and the heavy black leather boots, Liz would say that she moved like a ballet dancer, with an elegant glide across the floor. Effortless with a straight spine and her head held high. If there was a look that said 'soft butch', this woman rocked it. Liz stood up.

"Ms Zendeli?

"Ms Whitten. Please call me Beth." Her voice swept over Liz's skin and a faint tingle ran across the back of her neck, almost like… lust? Huh, she never felt that when she didn't know someone, therefore she dismissed the possibility. It must be a result of the awkward knowledge that this meeting was ill-advised.

"I'm Liz. Please have a seat."

"Thanks. And thank you for granting me this meeting. I really appreciate it." Up close, Beth had richly coloured brown eyes with faint crow's feet at the edges, and her black hair was sprinkled with grey around her ears. The salt and pepper was barely perceptible thanks to the close shave. It was difficult to judge her age; she could be anywhere between mid-thirties and late fifties, depending on how exacting her skin care regime was.

"Shall we get directly to the point?"

"Sure. It's simple. I've been a tenant in that building for over twelve years, and I've always paid my rent on time. I rent the whole thing; the ground floor for Seraph's Burlesque Club, and the upper floor has two apartments. I live in one, and my bartender Steph and her husband Walter, who is also our security manager, live in the other."

"None of that is new information." Liz was harsher than she would normally be. She couldn't let this lovely woman interrupt her plans.

"No, I imagine it's not. I expect that you'd have done your homework on my business." The woman analysed her with her gaze, with an intensity that Liz wasn't accustomed to. It was ... interesting. "Which is why I would like to know why you'd evict a long term tenant who always pays the rent on time, and who has recently completed vast improvements to the building."

"Improvements that are your responsibility as part of the lease agreement."

"I have run this business for a long time." The sarcasm was probably deserved. When Beth paused, Liz leaned forward in her seat, a sucker for punishment. "I understand the value in creating an atmosphere that attracts clientele."

The pesky sympathy that she'd felt when she'd gone to Drag Trivia grabbed her again. "Unfortunately for you, nothing will change my mind."

"Oh?" Disappointment washed over Beth's features for a moment, then disappeared as she leaned forward. Beth's face was now close enough to her own that Liz could feel her soft breath.

"I've done some sums and I'm willing to increase my rental payments."

Liz didn't budge. She pinned Beth with as fierce a gaze as she could manage. "I plan to knock down the building and create a five-storey apartment block. I doubt your increase in rent can compete with the projected profits from my plans."

Beth paled and shifted back in her seat. "I see."

"Yes. I'm sorry to waste your time." Liz needed to put some distance between them. She needed to leave now before she made this worse.

"I doubt that."

"Excuse me?"

"I don't think you are sorry at all. It takes a special type of arsehole to agree to a meeting and not even pretend to listen to my case."

Liz stared, unable to speak for a moment at the emotional display. Normally, something like that would make it easy to dismiss someone. Not this time. That bloody feeling that she was wrong grew in her gut and she tamped it down. "It's business, not friendship. You'll find somewhere else."

"Yes, but that's hardly the point, is it? You've given me a month to get out, while you plan to knock down the whole building. How long does planning permission take? Why not let me stay until you have the proper construction permissions for your grand fu... um, grand apartment block?"

Liz conceded that it made good sense to continue to have income during the planning process. "Sure. I'll get my lawyers to put that in writing, but you will be leaving when I need you to. I've done this many times and planning won't take much longer than six weeks, so you've bought yourself maybe two extra weeks."

"Every day matters when I need to manage a change on this scale, so thank you."

Liz got the impression that it took Beth quite a bit of effort to add that forced thanks at the end and she nearly chuckled at the way Beth's expression showed she wasn't impressed by the concession at all.

"Look, I know you think I'm a hard business person with no care for you or your club, but it's not true."

"There's no proof of any truth in that statement."

"Are you always so prickly?"

"Only to people who threaten my business and my home."

Liz probably deserved that. "I am sorry."

"I don't believe you. If you were sorry, you'd discuss options with me."

"No. Two things can exist in parallel. I can feel empathy for your plight, while also wanting to follow through with my plans."

"So my business is to be an unfortunate side effect of your grand design? Nice." Beth didn't hold back and Liz found herself admiring her. To survive in business for so long took backbone and Beth seemed to have plenty of it.

"Yes. The risk when you rent is that the landlady can make decisions that you have no say in."

A muscle on Beth's jaw clenched but she didn't drop her gaze. Her brown eyes were filled with fire.

"I'm sorry. I have another meeting at seven. It's been fascinating to meet you. Please take my card and email me with a full proposal. We can negotiate via email." Liz slid her card across the table and stood up. She was grateful that the Monty Don fiasco was going to start soon, because she needed an excuse to leave before she conceded everything to this feisty attractive woman. Beth. Such a soft sounding word for all that energy.

Liz walked out of the café quickly, using her phone to book a car as she moved away from the most interesting character she'd met in a long time. The meeting had surprised her; no, not the meeting itself. She was surprised and fascinated by Beth. She'd always been a sucker for a determined woman. Given the circumstances, it was unlikely that they'd ever become friends. Such a shame. The tightness in her chest reminded her of the same feeling she'd had when she first walked into Seraph's Burlesque Club— Beth's club—and maybe those two things were connected in some way.

Where the hell was QueenB? It was quarter past seven. Monty Don had been talking for fifteen minutes already and the comments were out of control. She'd already had to give Mrs Green a half hour block for more inappropriate sexual comments about Mr Don's hands; and she was struggling to read fast enough to keep on top of everything.

NotTheQueen: Where are you?

A minute later, she got the answer.

QueenB: Sorry. I had a meeting. It went longer than I expected and then traffic was shit.

NotTheQueen: Must have been a good meeting.

QueenB: No.

NotTheQueen: Want to talk about it?

Liz was still buzzing from her meeting with Beth. It was

such a pleasure to meet someone who knew their worth and wouldn't back down even when cornered. She really respected that. Could she incorporate Beth's business into her project somehow? She needed a concrete plan before she said anything, and right now, she was distracted by overly enthusiastic gardeners with a million questions for a famous gardener. Even people who were usually sensible, like BensGran84, were losing all common sense and gushing.

QueenB: Now?

NotTheQueen: Yeah, I banned Mrs Green already and everyone else is just gushing happily.

QueenB: Her obsession with his hands is pretty wild.

Liz sent a gif of someone's hands twirling around and around.

NotTheQueen: Everyone else has been well behaved. Excited but not rude.

QueenB: Nothing like a famous gardener to get everyone fangirling!

NotTheQueen: Tell me about it. Liz chuckled at the hundreds of comments flooding the section under the online live video of Monty Don. She should be highlighting the questions for Monty Don's assistant to find and answer, but whatever. The assistant was being paid for this. She was just a volunteer, and her friend sounded defeated. Oh, she should ask about the meeting, not just make a throw away comment about the current heightened emotions of a fandom going wild. Friendship mattered more than admin duties.

NotTheQueen: Your meeting, I mean.

QueenB: Where do I start? It seemed her friend already

interpreted her saying in a way that was hopefully conducive to her opening up.

NotTheQueen: The beginning…

QueenB: Remember I told you that the building I rent has just been sold. Yeah, well I just met with the new landlady to try and strike a deal after she threatened to evict my club. Scratch that, not threatened. Is evicting me. It's crappy timing. We recently renovated the whole place with this cool 1920s burlesque vibe.

Liz read the DM twice as the truth slowly seeped in. How on earth was she going to tell QueenB/Beth that she was the landlady pushing her out of her home and business? How had they been friends for so long without Liz knowing what Beth did for a job? It was dislocating to know she'd met her online friend in real life without knowing they knew each other. And now too much time had passed without her response. She had to say something, but what?

NotTheQueen: Hi Beth. I'm Liz and this is incredibly awkward.

QueenB: WTF?

NotTheQueen: Yeah. If I'd known, I wouldn't have bought the building.

QueenB: It's a bit late for that now. Why not just change your plans and leave me to run my business in peace? For friendship's sake.

NotTheQueen: It's tempting

QueenB: So be tempted. Fuck. We've been friends for a couple of years and now I get the shitty news that you are ruining my life.

Liz's eyes burned. She wasn't ruining anyone's life by buying a building and constructing something better. It might suck for Beth, but it would be better for more people in the long run. She pressed her thumbs against her nose and breathed in and out slowly.

NotTheQueen: It's not that dramatic

QueenB: It is. Seraph's is my life.

NotTheQueen: You can move. You have that power.

QueenB: Ok, property guru. Do you know how impossible it is to find a space big enough for my business, at an affordable rate, that also has good access to the tube and plenty of foot traffic? This location is a fucking unicorn and I don't want to leave.

NotTheQueen: Now you understand why I bought the building. Which you could have done.

QueenB: Ouch. Not everyone can afford London prices.

Liz knew that. To hear it from Beth felt like being stabbed in the back, and yet she knew she was the one doing the stabbing here.

NotTheQueen: Can we agree to disagree on this one?

It was a pathetic attempt to soothe their friendship and as soon as she hit send, Liz wanted to pull it back.

QueenB: No

Was it wrong that Liz adored having an adversary with such snarky strength? Probably.

NotTheQueen: I'm your friend, Beth.

QueenB: It doesn't feel like that right now. You, quite literally, hold an incredible amount of power over my life. And it would be easy for you to simply be my landlady and let me be.

NotTheQueen: You want me to give up my own dreams for yours?

Those little dots came and went. Liz wanted to know what Beth was typing, then deleting, then typing again. Were her own dreams really that important? Yes, they were.

She had a point to prove and it didn't involve conceding ground to someone, simply because she liked them. Especially if she liked them.

QueenB: One of us needs to compromise here if we both value this friendship. You have all the power and so I think it should be up to you to move further.

NotTheQueen: Understood

Liz understood what Beth was saying, but she wasn't about to explain to Beth why she couldn't give her what she wanted. She needed to step away from her computer and figure this out, like a big puzzle that she was trying to solve without all the pieces. Tonight's session with Monty Don couldn't end soon enough. She clicked away from her DMs and focused on sorting through the comments.

5

Beth quickly scanned the comments under the Monty Don video. There was nothing that needed intervention, so she logged off and went downstairs to her club. NotTheQueen—Liz—could deal with it all. God, she couldn't even begin to work out how she felt—uptight, frustrated, fucking angry—at the revelation that her friend was fucking her over. She needed to do something physical. She needed to fuck someone and feel them come around her fingers, or better yet, she needed someone to fuck her hard until she screamed. Luckily it was a Friday night, the club should be pumping and that always meant there was someone who would be keen to head upstairs to her flat with her.

As she stepped out into the noisy club, she made a sudden decision. Spite was probably a daft reason to make a management decision, but too bad. Tonight, she was going to make Jonti into a proper chef—like he was qualified to be —not just a kitchen hand who churned out bar snacks and cheese platters. He should be working with his qualifications properly, not simply being grateful for any work. They were going to open a full service, and he was going to run the whole thing. She had a feeling that he'd make a spectacular menu that would draw in more customers; people would arrive earlier and stay longer, spending more on drinks if they had decent food too. They were all going to be out on the streets in six weeks, maybe eight if they were lucky. They would go out with a bang, not a whimper. Her vague idea to improve the food at Seraph's had become something concrete. Beginning now.

"Beth. How did the meeting go?" Ben asked. He appeared from nowhere, startling her.

"Why aren't you back stage?" Fuck, she sounded bitchy tonight. Beth hauled in a deep breath. This mess belonged firmly in Liz's court. Beth wouldn't—shouldn't—take it out on anyone else, especially not her very friendly, shy, IT geek.

"I take it the meeting went badly, then? Did I do the wrong thing in setting it up?"

Beth shook her head. "No. It's not your fault, and I'm glad I went. I managed to negotiate an extra two weeks, which is shit, but better than nothing."

"Was the new landlady difficult?"

"Yes."

"Sounds like you took a knife to a gun fight."

Beth laughed cynically. "No. I went to a fucking picnic with chocolate cake as a gift, and they turned it into a gun fight."

"Ouch."

"I guess I shouldn't have expected a property investor to actually care about people, so that's on me." Beth hated the defeated note in her voice, but fucking hell, Liz had been her

34

friend online for a long time. They'd got each other through the tough times of a lockdown, through good humour and just being there to talk to whenever Beth felt lonely. And now, to discover her 'friend' was a hard-hearted property investor with the power to make her homeless… Beth felt betrayed and hurt and she wanted to lash out at Liz, at everyone, and at the whole bloody world. All the work and heartache that she'd sunk into Seraph's were about to be taken away by someone she thought was her friend. It wasn't fair. Hmph. Okay. It was time to put on her big girl pants and stop feeling sorry for herself. Life wasn't fair—experience had taught her that lesson—and she could survive whatever was thrown her way; even a betrayal of friendship like this.

"I'm sorry."

"Thanks. We'll figure out something. We have six weeks to make as much money as we can to get us through the next phase. You guys know that I'll look after all of you, don't you?"

"Beth. Families look after each other. We are here for you as well." Ben reached around her with his long arms and gave her an awkward hug. Damn it, she wouldn't cry. She held her breath until the prickles in her eyes went away and her stomach stopped churning, then patted Ben on the shoulder.

"Thanks. It'll be fine. I'll make sure of it." And she'd deal with the loss of her friendship separately. Honestly if Liz found it so easy to stab her in the back, then the friendship wasn't as solid as Beth had assumed. First things first; she needed to find Jonti and discuss the new menu and dining options. He'd only worked here for a few days so it was going to be a shock. A necessary one. Having something positive to plan for would help get her through the parts of this process that were going to suck.

A fter a couple of hours helping out behind the bar, Beth eventually made it to the kitchen where she outlined her plans to Jonti.

"We should do a pop-up restaurant," Jonti said.

"How would that work?"

"It's a temporary menu where short-term is the appeal. All the good chefs hold them, often in unusual places, as marketing tools for their restaurants."

"And you think this will work here?"

"Yes. I mean, I'm a nobody, but I have worked with some famous chefs back home, so we could use that in our marketing."

Beth nodded. "Our team can make you sound like someone interesting, imported directly from the USA."

"I came here for the free health care, but sure." Jonti smiled.

Beth couldn't ignore the comment about America's unimaginably bad health care system. "I'm glad you are here. If you need help navigating the system over here, one of our dancers, Yolande, works as a nurse in her day job."

"Thanks. I'm good. I don't need anything, it's more the principle of the matter. Plus I met my wife online, she's from Yorkshire, and I actually came here for her. I had no idea about the hospital stuff until I got here. It's funny how you get used to a screwed up system and don't realise that it could be different."

"I'm glad you are here. Having a proper chef is going to take Seraph's to the next level." Even if it was just temporary, Beth was looking forward to finally expanding the menu options at Seraph's.

Jonti's smile grew. "Thank you for giving me this chance. We should definitely market this as a pop-up restaurant with a one-off menu. It'll get all foodies here."

"Ok. There's just one catch."

"If it's about budget, I can work with anything."

"No. It's timing. The building has been sold and the new landlady has given us six weeks to move out." Maybe eight if they were lucky. How long did all the building approvals take anyway? Eight weeks sound ridiculously fast.

"That's shit."

"Yeah. So, can we get this happening for the next six weeks? Try and make a pile of money and then we'll have a bit of a buffer for when we move."

Jonti nodded. "Leave it with me. What's my budget?"

"How about you come up with a couple of options and I'll see what we can manage? Make a proper budget with costs and projected income."

The joy on Jonti's face pulled her out of her misery. "Thank you so much. I'm going to take this opportunity and make it fly."

"Great." Beth grinned back at him. She would add in a bonus payment to him, a profit sharing system, once he'd come up with the base budget. She walked back to the bar with only one thing left to do; get rid of all this pent up energy by getting fucked by someone. Anyone. The club always had a few lesbian or bisexual women who came to watch the show, hoping to pick up afterwards. All she needed right now was someone with plenty of energy. It'd obviously been too long since she'd had sex—two goddamn weeks—so she pushed off the wall and walked into the club.

"What the hell is she doing here?" Beth muttered under her breath. Liz sat at the bar, nursing what looked like a Breakfast Old Fashioned. Shouldn't she still be online, doing the Monty Don stuff? On the stage, Yolande was performing her 1930s dance with the crooning sounds of Louis Armstrong's What a Wonderful World as her backing tune. How dare Liz be here? And worse, drinking one of Beth's favourites. Smokey bourbon with dried orange peel that came together with rich flavours, warming the mouth and chest.

"Who?" Steph had magical bartender hearing. She could pick out anything anyone said—an incredibly useful skill when she ran the bar at Seraph's.

"Just someone I thought was a friend."

"But isn't?"

"It's hard to stay friends with someone who… Never mind." Beth poured herself a nip of bourbon and threw in a couple of rocks of ice. She almost added the dried orange peel but stopped herself. Pettiness won. There was no way she'd drink the same thing as Liz tonight. She'd been too upset during the meeting with Liz to notice how gorgeous she was.

Beth had always had a thing for older women. Her Jewel had been ten years older than her, a gap that had seemed huge when they'd first met and Beth was only twenty-five. Jewel Tran had been so worldly and protective and experienced; everything Beth had needed and desired then. The only similarity between Jewel and Liz was the same fierce flash in their eyes that Beth was a sucker for, something she looked for in all her hook ups.

Liz looked like a Scottish highlander, dark brown hair, blue eyes, pale skin covered in freckles, with a body built for walking up and down hills all day. Beth could easily imagine Liz's cheeks pink from the wind, or pink from sex, with her hair splayed over Beth's pillow. Bloody hell. She didn't even want to fuck Liz, her friend, her fucking land-lady from hell, or whatever the heck they were to each other now. Beth bit her bottom lip. Even as she thought all of this, she knew the truth deep down. She hated the way Liz did business, except that she loved the way Liz stuck to her goals. She wanted to have Liz on her side, to protect her, rather than screw her over. Imagine—just imagine—having all that power supporting her. The only problem was that she was the one getting fucked over, and now she had to deal with the added complication of feeling a physical attraction to Liz.

"Good crowd tonight."

"Yeah." Beth had already noticed that all the tables were filled, and the attention was almost all on Yolande, who finished with a flourish. The audience cheered. Charlie appeared from the wings and grabbed the microphone. Beth let Charlie's chatter thanking Yolande and introducing the next dancer wash over her as she sipped her bourbon. There would be a break soon, and the bar would get busy. It usually went in waves, quiet while one of the dancers was on stage, then busy between acts.

"While I've got you, Steph."

"Yeah?"

"We are going to run a pop-up restaurant for the next six

weeks. Jonti, the new kitchen hand, is actually a trained chef, so I want to utilise his skills better."

"That'll be awesome. So we'd open earlier for the foodie crowd, then roll into our usual evenings?"

"I think so. We need to sit down and work out the details." Beth would need to think about ticketing options. She glanced over at Liz again. The urge to march up to her and ask her what the fuck she was doing in Beth's club grew until she had no option. She tipped the rest of her drink down her throat, needing the burn on the way down, and placed the glass with the rest of the dirty glasses. Before she could doubt herself, she'd marched around the bar and through the room until she stood in front of Liz.

"What do you think you are doing here?"

"I was hoping to see you."

"What about Monty Don?"

"His assistant had it all under control. Our conversation ended in an unsatisfactory manner, so I was hoping to see you here and resolve some of that."

"You can't expect me to continue to be your friend, Liz, or NotTheQueen, or whatever."

Liz blinked once. "I can. We've come to a reasonable solution with regards to this place. I want to know why you are still angry at me."

"Shockingly, I'm not keen to be friends with someone who callously boots me out of my home and livelihood." Two extra weeks was hardly a reasonable solution. "You can't paint yourself as some kind of benefactor here just because you've given me more time to move out of my home." Beth wanted to fight—or fuck—and Liz's calm logical only made that need worse.

"I've been more than fair. Another buyer might not give you the same options."

"Another buyer might not knock down the whole bloody building either. Another buyer might see the good sense in keeping a tenant who always pay the rent on time, even during a fucking pandemic."

Liz flinched and Beth hated how much she liked that. Was she a shit person for wanting to paint Liz as her enemy? No, she just needed to keep Liz at a distance.

"Your exemplary record as a tenant is the main reason why I'm happy to entertain alternatives."

"Giving me two extra weeks hardly makes you a benevolent dictator."

Liz laughed. Actually laughed at her, and Beth clenched her hands into fists at her sides. She would not punch her new landlady.

"Why is that funny?" Beth asked. "Not much about this situation is funny."

"I don't want to be a dictator over your life. The concept doesn't align with reality. I just want to be your friend, Beth."

"Then don't knock down my building. I've worked bloody hard to build this business, and it's my home. You need to see that it's not an inconvenience to me. This matters."

"Understood."

"That's the second time you've said that, but I don't believe you. I don't think you understand at all."

"Then explain it to me," Liz said.

"Not here." Beth was working. "Enjoy the evening." She walked away before she did something wild, like punch Liz or kiss her. Hate sex would be perfect right now. She joined Steph behind the bar and distracted herself by talking to customers. Hard work would get her through this confusing patch of emotions and later, when she was alone, she'd pull out some of her favourite toys and give her body some release too. It would be unfair to ask a real person to soothe all this rage.

6

"Liz. Come in." Gita opened the door and welcomed her inside her home. Liz handed over the bottle of wine she'd brought, then slipped off her shoes, and sanitised her hands. The habit had formed during the pandemic and now it'd become normal, as the idea of bringing in any germ from outside to a friend's house seemed wrong. She sat down at her usual spot in the kitchen and watched as Gita poured wine for the three of them.

"Harlan, how have you been?"

"Great." Gita's husband stirred a small pot of something. "I hope you like roast beef with all the trappings. It's perfect for a cool evening."

"You know I do." Liz smiled. "Nothing like a good roast with Yorkshire puds and gravy and a beer after a long walk on a rainy day."

"Well, I can't supply the walk or the rain, but the rest is here."

Gita passed her a glass of wine. "Thanks for inviting us

to the Drag Trivia. It was awesome fun. We should absolutely do that again."

Had it already been a couple of weeks since that night? Liz sipped her wine, then placed the glass back on the bench with an unsteady hand.

"Yeah, about that…"

"What have you done?"

"Why do you assume I've done something?" Liz shook her head at Harlan, who winked at her. "Fine. I guess you guys know me too well."

"There was something in your tone…" Harlan said.

"I feel like the worst kind of dickhead."

"Oh? You know I was just kidding."

"What's the matter?" Gita rushed around the kitchen bench and slung her arms around Liz's shoulders.

"Please don't judge me."

"We would never." Gita paused for a moment. "It's not like you to say that."

"Fine." The joy and frustration of a long term friendship was how well they knew her. "I'm judging myself and it's not great."

"Stop that. This is a safe space for you to air your grievances."

Liz chuckled at the nineties sitcom reference. "I'm hardly going to bring out the… what was it? Festivus pole?"

"Yeah, my favourite Seinfeld episode."

Harlan leaned on the kitchen counter and stared at them both. "Okay, but now you are just avoiding the issue. What happened?"

Liz sighed. "You know the plant group I'm in online?"

"Yeah. Did you get into a fight with someone over a cactus or something?"

"Harlan! No, but one of the other admins is a good friend of mine and I've just learned that she rents one of my buildings."

Harlan made an odd sound and Gita hugged her tighter.

"Oh dear. Are you worried about that? If she's your friend, she's not going to take advantage of you. Not everyone is Petunia."

Liz closed her eyes. It would be easy to protest that the situation with Petunia had occurred years ago and the sourness of that relationship had no bearing on her life now, but she could see the parallels, except…

"I'm worried that I'm the Petunia in this situation."

"What? How do you figure?"

It should be easier to admit this to her friends, but she couldn't get the conversation with Beth out of her head. After the awkward introduction online and the argument they'd had, she'd gone to the club to try and make things better. It'd only made things worse. Why couldn't Beth understand that it wasn't personal? Her plans had nothing to do with their friendship. If anything, her plans were more about proving to herself that she wasn't going to let Petunia win.

"Okay, so it's not exactly the same, but um, I sent her an eviction notice…"

"What? You can't evict a friend." Gita pulled away from the hug.

"Liz, that's not like you," Harlan said.

She held her hands up in front of her. "I thought this was a safe space."

"It is." Gita hugged her again. "What happened? I'm guessing it's more complicated than you are letting on."

Liz sighed. "I didn't know she was my friend when I sent the notice."

"How does that work?"

"Gita. Online friendships don't always include real life information." Harlan played a lot of online games so he probably understood.

"Yes, we've been friends online since the pandemic began, but I only knew her by her user name. And then I bought this building and evicted the tenants because I'm going to build something better. It wasn't until after I evicted her that I realised she was my online friend."

"Awkward."

"Yes, sooo awkward. And…" Could Liz admit this? Yes, these were her friends. "I really like her. I feel conflicted about this."

"Can you un-evict her?" Harlan asked.

Liz nodded. "Yes."

"But?" Gita must have heard her think it.

"But I have plans for the site and I—" She wasn't sure how to articulate it. Everyone waited for her. Gita paced around the room for a while, something Liz understood because they'd met at a rambling club and moving helped with thinking.

"Just because Petunia treated you like a bank account, doesn't mean that everyone will. Your friend isn't going to take advantage if you concede the space a little. Friendship matters more than money in the end."

She growled at the memory of Petunia, even though she'd already thought it herself. "I don't want to talk about

Petunia, who is old news and not relevant here. All I want is to fix a friendship."

"Have you tried… I don't know… talking to her." The grin on Gita's face was so smug, it jerked Liz out of her funk a little, but Gita's usual teasing nonsense didn't really help because she'd landed on one of the problems.

"Last time I tried that, it just made it worse."

"You mean, she didn't appreciate being told that you were going to make her homeless."

"Oh for fuck's sake, Gita." Liz let her frustration out and was gratified when Harlan sent Gita a look of caution. "I'm not making my friend homeless. Why does everyone want to pretend I'm some heartless business owner?"

"Liz. I'm just playing devil's advocate."

"Every time someone says that, it's usually just an excuse to be mean." Liz swallowed her pride. "I'm sorry."

"Don't be sorry. We've been friends for a long time, and I hate to see you so conflicted like this. There's obviously something about this online friend of yours that is confusing you."

"Yes. Very confusing." The relief in having Gita notice that was palpable.

"Liz. We love you, and we know how much Petunia hurt you. I know, I know. It was a long time ago, but obviously this situation has some parallels, even though it's only a friendship on the line. It's okay to be worried about not ending up in a similar situation again."

Liz drank her wine and glanced at Harlan. "Are there really similarities?"

"Only you can answer that." Harlan provided spectacularly unhelpful advice, although…

"Okay." Liz sucked in a deep breath. "I'm worried that if I un-evict Beth, then I'll be doing the same thing I always did with Petunia. Giving in to her needs and ignoring mine. I don't want to put her needs before my goals."

"It doesn't have to be so black and white though. Is there a way you can both get what you want?"

Liz shook her head. "I don't know. I want change and Beth doesn't. But I'm torn. She's a really good friend, who helped me a lot during the long lockdowns when I couldn't get out and walk."

"Hey!" Gita laughed.

"You guys were great too, and we shared the same frustrations, but Beth and the plant group gave me a new hobby. Learning to grow plants indoors helped bring greenery and the outdoors close to me when I couldn't get out. I really value that."

"But not enough to want to give up your own goals." Harlan hit the nail on the head.

"It's a dilemma for sure. You don't want to upset your friend, and you feel the need to repay her for her friendship and help during the lockdowns, but you also don't want to fall into the same old patterns that you had with Petunia." Gita outlined it all quite well.

"Basically, yes. If I give up my goals with the property, then I haven't learned anything from that old mess. But if I don't, I risk losing a good friend."

"Perhaps there is a middle ground, another solution that will allow you to get your goals and still help your friend?" Harlan asked.

"Yeah, like you could offer her rent in another one of your properties." Gita grinned.

"Sure." Talking about Petunia always made her stomach churn. Liz changed the subject. "When is dinner? It smells amazing, Harlan."

"About half a glass of wine away." Harlan turned to stir the gravy again.

Gita hugged her again. "I'm sorry for pushing so hard before. This is obviously a tricky situation for you."

"Sometimes, Gita, you can be a little condescending."

"And you can be stubborn, and we love each other anyway." Gita squeezed her a bit tighter then walked over to fuss with the table setting. Seeing Gita trying so hard to make her feel comfortable always warmed Liz's heart. Her friend might be a little abrupt at times, but she was kind and meant well.

"How's work going, Gita?"

Gita grinned. "Yeah, really great. I signed a new show this week." Gita worked for a major television producer making children's programs.

"Well done. I'm proud of you."

Harlan cheered. "Time for dinner, champions."

"Champions?"

"Yeah, Gita with her new show and you with a new building. I just hope I've made a dinner worthy of celebration."

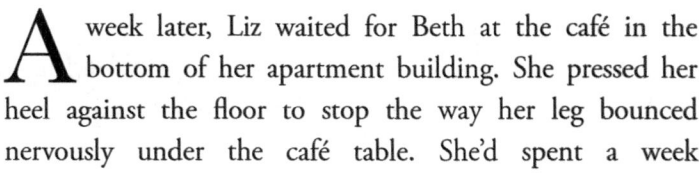

A week later, Liz waited for Beth at the café in the bottom of her apartment building. She pressed her heel against the floor to stop the way her leg bounced nervously under the café table. She'd spent a week researching alternative locations for Beth's club and now they were meeting to discuss them. In terms of suitability, each option met all of Beth's criteria bar one. It would be up to Beth to decide which part she wanted to compromise on and that would determine which choice she made for the club.

"Hi." Beth slid into the seat opposite her. She wore the same brown leather jacket from their last meeting, paired with a jaunty purple shirt today and tight black jeans with the same black leather boots.

"Hello. Would you like to order first?"

"I'm here for business, Liz, not for socialising." Beth's brown eyes flashed with determination.

"We can do both. I want to remain friends with you." Liz tried to ignore the clammy sweat on the palms of her hands. This shouldn't be so important. Liz had plenty of friends, she could afford to lose one along the way, except she didn't want to lose Beth. She, especially, didn't want to rationalise this as a transaction, or worry about the parallels to history. All week, she'd missed the happy banter with Beth in the Plant Parent group, logging in each day in the hope of a DM from QueenB only to find silence. It wasn't the same without her friend.

"Sometimes we don't get what we want. Like, I want to keep my club in its excellent location, and you want to build some ugly concrete apartment building and make money. One of us isn't going to get what we want."

"I'm sorry."

"Shall we focus on business?" Beth sighed. "It's all I have the bandwidth for at the moment." She did look quite tired, and Liz noticed the extra concealer under Beth's eyes and a pinched expression on her mouth.

"Let me order you lunch. What would you like?"

"Just a salad. I'm not allergic to anything, so whatever." It must be her dancer training because Beth sat ramrod straight even though she looked like she needed to sag exhaustedly into a hug. A hug? Liz stood up quickly before she gave that thought too much attention and walked to order their lunch. She ordered two different types of salad; a Caesar salad and a Thai papaya salad. Beth could have whichever one she liked and Liz would take the other. The food here was always good, fresh and consistent. She ordered two lattes as well, then went back to sit down. Beth had leaned back in her chair, sitting with her ankle resting on the knee of her other leg, and she was flicking over stuff on her phone.

"I got you a latte too. I don't know if you drink coffee, but I thought it might be good." Liz paused. "Um, because this is a business meeting and you know coffee is the fuel of business."

Beth put her phone down, screen-side down which Liz appreciated. "Did you just make a joke?"

"Yes?" Liz didn't want her pulse to race nervously like this. They used to joke all the time about stuff online, and it had been easy. Simple. Fun. Now their relationship was tense and awkward, and she didn't know what to do about it. She'd created this tension, and she wanted to fix it, more than she ought.

"And you bought me a latte? Don't tell me you are one of those property investors who tell everyone they just need to be careful with their money. Drink less lattes, then you'll be able to get a start in the property market. It's not the smashed avocado on toast that is the problem."

Liz met Beth's glare and tried to keep her expression softer. "I know how hard it is to get into the London property market."

"Okay." Was that a concession from Beth? "Every single one of those articles written about how some perky young kid became a property guru has a one liner hidden in the text about the person getting a leg up from their wealthy parents." Perhaps not. Beth continued to glare at her.

"Unfortunately, having that financial assistance is necessary to get a foothold in this market."

"I hope you acknowledge your privilege."

"I do." Liz knew it, but it was also complicated and she hoped Beth was still enough of a friend to understand. "My parents died when I was twenty. I inherited their house and yes, some people might say I was lucky to have that unfortunate event start my property portfolio, but that overlooks the pain of being orphaned." Liz hadn't shared that with many people, only close friends. Before all this mess, she had considered Beth to be one of her close friends. Putting aside the current tension between them, she wanted to maintain that connection, which was why she wanted Beth to understand why her plans mattered so much. Her parents had been doctors, they'd both believed that everyone deserved to live in a healthy, clean house. They'd literally lived their beliefs and had died during a cyclone in Haiti while working for an international charity. Her investments honoured their lives and deeds. Petunia had nearly destroyed it all, and it'd taken her years to rebuild her portfolio.

"I'm sorry about your parents."

"It's a long time ago. The grief softens with time. Obviously some things are always going to be tricky, but I've been alive longer without them than I was with them." Liz lived a simple life compared to her parents who'd lived for action and had used their medical knowledge to help people. Every one of Liz's fifty commercial properties had space reserved for charitable organisations with cheap rent so they could focus on the work they did. It wasn't the same as doing the work, of course, but it wasn't an insignificant contribution either. She hoped her parents would be proud of her. She vetted each charity carefully to check their ratio of spend on administration vs the spend on their goals and outreach. Too many charities spent a high portion of their income on administration and advertising to get more income, which often meant they were well-meaning without being useful.

"It does. Grief, I mean."

"You are an orphan too?"

Beth closed her eyes and breathed out slowly. "No. My partner, Jewel, died in a car accident thirteen years ago."

"Oh, I'm so sorry to hear that."

"She is the reason why the club is so important to me." Beth delivered that with a defiant stare, one that hit Liz like an emotional punch to the stomach. Liz admired the way Beth stuck to her principles. It wasn't often she met someone who could match her for determination. Heat trickled down her spine and her nipples tightened a little. Weird.

"I've had a look through my portfolio and could suggest a few spaces for you to rent if you like."

"Your portfolio?"

"Of properties. I own several commercial properties, and I'm sure I can accommodate Seraph's Burlesque Club in one of them." Liz had forty-nine others to pick from and she would've started sorting through them except Beth cleared her throat in a way that almost sounded like she was covering up an accidental comment. She held Liz's gaze.

"I won't pay a cent more in rent and would like to negotiate a discount given the upheaval you intend to put my business through."

Liz almost smiled. Negotiating like this was fun. Suddenly the prospect of working together with Beth in the future beckoned with potential and all her earlier doubts about Petunia disappeared. Petunia had always agreed with her, always stroked her ego, while Beth was the opposite.

"I'm sure we can come to an arrangement."

Their salads arrived, saving Liz from saying what a relief it was to have provided a solution that would make Beth happy. And it was—a relief. No, more than that. She wanted to please Beth. Oh dear, that could only mean one thing. Somewhere in the depths of her demisexual brain, Liz was beginning to form an attraction to Beth. At nearly fifty years of age, she'd experienced this a few times, this slow understanding that revealed itself like the way the sun filtered faintly through the dense trees when hiking in the Cotswolds. Sometimes, friendship just stayed that way, and other times, like with Petunia, it evolved into something more. It'd been confusing when she was younger before the internet was so ubiquitous, but one day she'd learned the term demisexual and the whole world suddenly made so much more sense. She wasn't broken or weird because she didn't do insta-lust—the internet had given her that term too—she was just herself and like many others, she needed an emotional connection before she made a physical one.

They ate in silence; Beth had chosen the papaya salad, so Liz ate the Caesar salad. The cos lettuce was nice and crisp, and the dressing worked well with pepper on the eggs and bacon pieces to add a touch of heat.

"How is the salad?"

"Fine."

"Have I offended you somehow? I thought…"

Beth put her fork down, picked up a napkin, and dabbed at her mouth.

"Yeah. Look, even if I rent something else that you own, you are still going to be my landlady with the power to make me move again. Our friendship is going to have to be on pause."

"I'm sorry you feel that way." Liz had hoped offering Beth a place in one of her other buildings might patch up the friendship a little.

"Yeah, but what can be done about it?" Beth stood up, picked up Liz's carefully prepared portfolio with extensive notes on why each property would suit Beth's needs, and walked out leaving Liz with a strange prickle in her chest.

If she helped Beth move, maybe she would get a chance to explore the new physical responses she was having around Beth. She hadn't mentioned that to Gita and Harlan, mostly because she didn't completely know what she was feeling yet, and after the whole discussion around Petunia, the last thing she wanted was to listen to her well-meaning friend discuss her love life, or lack of it. It didn't really matter if Gita wanted her to fall in love, or if she was going to advise Liz to be cautious; either way it was not Gita's business. How odd. She didn't usually feel this need to keep something from her friends.

7

Beth tucked Liz's stupid portfolio brochure, or whatever the fuck it was, inside her motorbike trunk, put on her helmet, then slung her leg over the bike and turned on the 900CC engine with a roar. She checked the traffic and drove away from another pointless meeting with Liz. Why did she keep agreeing to meet her? It always ended up so unsatisfying. Beth couldn't help the hope that Liz would recognise their friendship and not be so hard nosed about everything.

Would it hurt Liz to give in a little? She owned enough properties to have a fucking portfolio for Beth to pick from, and honestly, even after Liz had tried to butter her up with lunch, Beth wasn't sure she wanted Liz as her long term land-lady. Not when she was so fucking stubborn. Liz appeared to have zero understanding of the impact of the financial power differential between them. Beth focused on guiding her bike safely through the traffic, and eventually parked her bike in its usual spot behind the club, before storming inside.

"Hey, how was the meeting?" Charlie looked way too cheerful.

"What a fucking waste of time." Beth dumped the portfolio on the desk she shared with Charlie. "We are still being evicted, but our landlady has offered us one of her other properties."

"Hopefully one has a decent location. I've been hunting online for something and all the options suck."

"I know." Beth had been obsessing over the rental market in the last month; and the lack of options was pretty much the only reason she'd agreed to meet Liz today, for all the good that'd done. That and pointless hope that their friendship meant something to Liz. Blergh.

"We are going to have to compromise on something. Either foot traffic, or size, or interiors."

"Yeah." And all the while, Liz missed the point and seemed to want to stay friends with her. It made no sense and was just generally infuriating. "I think we should compromise on interiors. With the right long term rental contract, we can do another refit."

"Elle would love that." Charlie gushed about her partner, who'd done the interior design for Seraph's recently. Charlie's joy was infectious, and Beth let it settle around her, glad for the positive energy. At this point, she'd grab it all, like a joy vampire sucking it away from others, which wasn't like her at all. This was all weighing a bit too heavily and she needed a resolution quickly before she exploded with pent up frustration.

"Let's plan for a refit. It might open up more options to us." Beth wanted to growl, but she forced herself to be sensible. "And we may as well look at Liz's places too, just in case there is something."

"If we think about our clientele and why they come here, and where they come from, that might narrow down the scope of location."

Beth rubbed her eyes. "Why didn't I think of that?" She should've done the basic research to know how far her clients travelled. "We have all the data from when we first opened up after the lockdowns because people had to book tickets online."

"Stress makes it hard to think logically. Don't beat yourself up, Beth."

Beth shook her head. "It's my business. I'm supposed to be all over that type of thing."

"You are only one person, Beth, and you spend so much time looking after us that I'm surprised you have any time for boring business shit."

Beth laughed. "Nice of you to prove that I've employed you in the correct job."

"What?"

"Relax. I'm not going to ask you to do boring business shit, as you call it. I'll figure out the data or get Ben to help me."

"Cool."

"Just focus on planning the next few weekends. And hey, talk to Jonti about how to tie your shows in with his pop-up restaurant. Let me stress about our landlady and where we are going to move to."

Beth was a bit confused by Liz; the old landlord hadn't bothered with meetings. Provided she'd paid the rent on time, he didn't seem to care, but then, this situation wasn't typical. She scrunched up her nose. It'd probably been a bad idea to open up to Liz online. Would she rather still be her friend, and not have this pressure of knowing she held Beth's livelihood in her hands? It wouldn't be complicated then. She'd have to move out and she'd do it; kicking and screaming as she went. Now she had the double whammy of having to move out and the grief of losing a friend. Ouch. Breaking up with a friend sucked, and when they held all the power over her life, it felt mean-spirited somehow.

"Speaking of Jonti, did you meet his wife, Gloria?"

"No. Did she drop by the club?"

"Yes. She's like super pregnant and had an appointment at the hospital near here."

Beth raised her eyebrow. "Super pregnant?"

"Huge and uncomfortable looking, poor thing. You'd never catch me doing that to my body."

Beth shook her head. "Charlie, no one is asking you to do that. Your body is yours."

Charlie wrinkled her nose and grinned. "I never really understood this need to have kids, and Elle agrees. I mean, it's pretty amazing that the human body can, like grow a whole other human inside them, but not for me. Like, we both have complicated families, so maybe that's why?"

Beth didn't want to think about it. She'd never had any interest in having kids and neither had Jewel. "I doubt it has anything to do with your parents. People just know what they want and that's it."

"Elle's family have been putting a lot of pressure on her brother's wife to have another kid, so I guess seeing Gloria today reminded me of that whole ugly mess."

"Wait. They aren't pressuring her brother, just the wife?

That's a bit fucked up."

Charlie nodded. "So fucked up. Elle is really stressed by it, and well, you know my mum and her current drama with the press over the revelation about my father." Charlie's mother, Lottie Alcott-James, acted in a long running soap opera, and Charlie was the result of a long ago affair with world famous actor Tom Scottridge. Tom had paid Charlie's mum to keep it a secret until recently when both her parents acted in the same movie and the truth was leaked to the media.

"Just because your parents are a mess and Elle's sound like misogynistic assholes, doesn't preclude you from having your own family."

"Elle and I are a family. We don't need children to do that." Charlie winked. "Beth, you should know better."

Beth grimaced. "As much as I like debating random topics with you Charlie, we have only three weeks left until we have to move out and I have a lot to organise." Changing the subject when she was wrong was a bit of a dick move, but it worked as Charlie gasped.

"Holy shit. We have so much crap to move."

"Yeah, all the costumes will have to be moved with care."

"And the bloody Mini! Why do we have so many things?"

Beth shrugged. "Moving sucks, but we may as well get used to the idea because three weeks isn't a very long time."

Charlie clapped her on the shoulder. "Well, if anyone can keep this club going, it's you. We survived a pandemic; a little move to a new location isn't going to keep us down."

"Team work. Let's get this happening." Beth sucked in a deep breath. It was time to find a new location—a better location—and preferably one that didn't have her ex-friend as a landlady.

8

L iz paced along the street, using her stride length to measure the width of the property that neighboured Seraph's Burlesque Club. Her agent and lawyers had sent a very generous offer to the owners, and she wanted to tell Beth about it. For some reason, she couldn't let go of this friendship. The need to fix things was greater than the alarm bells rung by Gita with her talk of how Petunia had treated her. Beth was nothing like Petunia, who'd been agreeable and pleasant. Petunia had sucked in Liz with a long game of niceness; Beth actively pushed Liz away and didn't want her help.

"What are you doing here?" Beth proved Liz's point with her surly tone. "Is it not enough that you are evicting me? You have to keep throwing it in my face by being here all the time."

"Beth, I'm sorry that you are hurting so much over this decision."

Beth shook her head. "You keep saying that. And yet, here you are. Again. You know what, forget it. I'm going to get some lunch." Beth checked the road for traffic, then marched across to the little sushi shop on the other side. The slight hitch in her elegant stride made Liz curious. Liz followed her across the street, and into the shop before she slid into a chair across the table from Beth.

"Can you leave me alone?"

"Would you grant me five minutes?"

Beth sneered. "Well, it's half the time you gave me when we first met. Seems fair."

"I have one idea that might work for both of us. I didn't want to say anything in case I couldn't pull it off." She really shouldn't get Beth's hopes up about this, but she had to do something to remove the devastation on Beth's face. Even since Beth had mentioned that she'd dedicated her club to her dead partner, guilt had plagued Liz. Guilt… and Gita's comment about finding a middle ground that worked for both of them. This confusing mess was why she didn't mix friendship with her work; except that wasn't even true as Sreesha rented one of her properties and it wasn't at all messy.

"Okay? I'm not sure I want to hear it. Your ideas haven't exactly been helpful so far." Beth didn't pull her punches and Liz knew she had to make this work if there was any chance in saving their friendship. Quite why she wanted that so much wasn't something she wanted to think too hard about, especially not while Beth sat there, glaring at her with those deeply intense brown eyes and gorgeous lips. If she rubbed her eyes, or blinked hard enough, hopefully she'd be less drawn to Beth.

"I've put in an offer for the two buildings next door to yours." It was a huge offer, far more than the properties were worth, and would push her debt profile into uncomfortable territory if—and that was a big if—the owners accepted the offer. She'd already worked out which of her other properties she could sell to keep her debt profile lower, so she'd only have to service the debt for a short time. The market was strong and interest rates were low. All up it was a reasonable gamble to make from a financial point of view, and if it helped resolve her friendship with Beth, then she'd take all the financial risk to make it happen.

Beth shrugged and Liz waited for her to speak, but she said nothing.

"If they accept my offer, I plan to do construction into two phases. I'll build next door first, so you can stay where you are, and then you can move next door into a purpose built new building before I knock down the one you are in now." The beauty of this plan was that Liz didn't have to compromise any part of her plans, and it had the added benefit of helping her friend, maybe even saving their friendship.

Beth just stared at her.

"I don't want to get your hopes up, but it's the best solution I can come up with that gets us both what we want."

"Do I get any say in the plans?"

"First things first, they need to accept my offer, so I don't think you should stop trying to find a new place to rent, but yes, obviously I want your input because the club will end up occupying the first new building."

"Okay. That works for me."

"Really?" Liz's heart fluttered with hope that she'd saved their friendship, and she almost cringed at herself. Was she the one who didn't want to get her hopes up here? Why was she so invested in Beth's well-being?

"Obviously it's a long shot, but if you can pull it off..." Beth's voice trailed away and then she grinned, "—then I'd be open to negotiating renting space in your ultra modern ugly concrete monstrosity."

Liz covered her mouth with her hand, so Beth couldn't see the huge smile that burst across her face. After a moment, the smile faded and she dropped her hand. "Excellent. And just so you know, it's not going to be an ugly concrete monstrosity."

"Glass then. Whatever."

"I want to create something like the Oasis of Aboukir in Paris and the UTS building in Sydney. Have you seen them?"

"No."

"They have massive vertical gardens as part of the building structure. I can go to five storeys high under the current zoning, and provided there aren't archaeological issues, I should be able to put three levels of carparking underneath."

"Would Seraph's get access to some of those carparks?"

"Anything is possible." Liz's leg started jiggling under the table. This was so exciting. "We can write something into our contract."

"Good. The location means that people don't need to drive to attend the club, however, it might be good to have at least one staff carpark, and a few reserved for VIP guests."

Liz wrote that down as a note in her phone. She didn't really need to, but it gave her something to do with her hands. "You mentioned in our last meeting that the club is your way of remembering your partner? Would you like to name one of the new buildings in her honour?"

Beth shook her head and Liz held her breath.

"Have I done something wrong?"

"No. Jewel didn't want me to start Seraph's. Her excuse was that the risk was too great, and I was too young to be able to properly manage a club like that. She wanted me to stop dancing because… Never mind, that's no one's business."

"It's okay, you don't need to share."

Beth tilted her head slightly. "I refused to give up something I loved. My mother is a dancer too; dancing is my whole life. Eventually Jewel came to understand that if she truly loved me, then she'd support my dancing too. We figured it out, but she thought the financial risk of having my own club was a step too much."

"I don't understand."

"It's complicated."

Liz wanted to rest her hand over Beth's to show she cared.

"I shouldn't even be telling you this."

"Please. We are friends."

Beth scoffed. "We were friends."

"I'd like to continue to be your friend. Please help me understand so I can…" She couldn't finish the sentence without giving away the beginnings of her feelings for Beth. Lustful feelings that were so new and tender that she wasn't ready to acknowledge them and besides one harsh comment would trample them. She knew from experience that she had to wait until she was sure before saying something, because people who weren't demisexual tended to charge forward before she was ready.

~

Beth couldn't believe that Liz would buy the fucking building next door and expand her project just so Seraph's could stay in the same place. As far as a gesture to save a friendship went, it was utterly compelling and incredible. She didn't want to trust it. Until today, Liz hadn't budged on her plan to evict Beth and knock down her building. To be fair, Liz was still going to do that, it was just that she'd expanded the demolition in a way that would benefit Beth too. The idea that Liz would spend more money to allow Beth to keep what she loved was seductive. She had spent half of this conversation biting her tongue, so she didn't blurt out something rude asking Liz just how much money she had. Asking that was easier than asking why Liz would go to such lengths for … their friendship.

"You want to understand why I am so determined to keep Seraph's?"

"Yes. I mean, I get the basics. It's your business. I wouldn't want to compromise on my own business either."

Beth raised her eyebrows deliberately. "I definitely know you wouldn't."

"Ha. Can we move on? I'd love to understand more about what you said about Jewel and, well, about what drives you to succeed."

Beth threw caution to the wind—her heart was still thumping happily at the notion that Liz had found a solution to Seraph's biggest problem—and besides, talking about

Jewel kept her memory alive. They'd had five wonderful years together before the car crash that had killed Jewel. Beth still had lunch with Jewel's mum, Yen, once a fortnight, more often than she saw her own parents. Yen needed the time together as much as Beth did.

"Jewel was driving that day. We argued about the club idea again. I'd been saving up and this building was for rent at a price I could afford. I had a whole plan and she dismissed it. She didn't want me to fail, and the odds were that the club would fail. She said I was too young."

"How old were you?"

"Thirty."

"What? I thought you were going to say nineteen." Liz's eyes widened and Beth had to laugh.

"Well, Jewel was older than me and it wasn't so much about the number. She said I wasn't ready to take the heartache that goes with putting everything into a venture and seeing it fail. A club had such a low chance of success. There was always a reason why I shouldn't do it."

Liz had a stunned expression on her face. "I hate to speak ill of the dead—"

"Stop." Beth held up her hand. "No good can come from finishing that sentence. I know I've painted her as quite negative about my goals. You need to know this; Jewel loved me. She said she was only protecting me and she was right. Running Seraph's was a lot tougher than I expected at first. A lot harder." Beth had barely slept for the first few months. She'd done everything; all the jobs that Charlie and Ben and Steph and Reiko did now. She'd been the MC on stage and the bar keeper and the kitty for the other dancers, and sourced all the dancers and created the shows, and managed a never-ending stream of mediocre kitchen hands and average bar staff. All while learning basic business skills like accounting and tax and payroll…

"There were a lot of skills I had to learn on the go, and I hadn't been prepared for how much time it would take. Jewel must have known that the club would take all my attention, and I'd have no energy for a relationship. She was wise like that."

"She sounds like she enjoyed your company."

"Yes, Jewel cared deeply."

"I'm sorry for misunderstanding."

Beth nodded. "Thanks. Anyway, we argued that day. She wasn't concentrating on the road and ran a red light. A truck ploughed into the car, right into Jewel. She died instantly and my leg was trapped. It took them ages to cut me free, and by then, it was too late. The foot couldn't be saved, it was too mangled and hadn't had enough blood flow."

"Beth. That's dreadful. You must know it wasn't your fault," Liz said.

"It was my fault. If I hadn't picked an argument with her while she was driving, she wouldn't have run that red light. Anyway…" Beth paused. "I'm pretty sure it makes me self-ish, but when I was released from hospital, I knew I had to start Seraph's because I couldn't dance anymore, and it was all I had left. It had been my dream and part of me needed to know if Jewel had been right. If I failed, then I'd always know that her death wasn't for nothing. I guess, grief is a strange motivator. It didn't matter anymore to win the argument. A large part of me wanted Seraph's to fail when I first started; it would be justice served, but in the end, I realised I was kidding myself and I needed to succeed for my own sake."

"And you needed somewhere to expend all your energy?"

"Yes. I had a small insurance payment after the accident and used it to rent the space and do a basic refit. Eventually I realised that Seraph's was the risk I had to take to figure out who I was without being able to dance. I like to think that Jewel would be proud of me. She had her doubts and sometimes, especially in those early years, I wanted her to be right, but I'm still here, and Seraph's is still open. She always smiled when she said I was stubborn."

"And I threatened everything you worked for." Liz's face softened and for a second Beth thought Liz might cry.

"Not just that. You were my friend and you refused to even try and help me. It was a kick to the guts."

"That makes a lot of sense. I'm sorry."

"Thanks." Beth hated that it took for her to open up her heart and tell her sob story to get what she wanted, and she didn't fully trust Liz's new plans since there was too much resting on whether the neighbour would sell or not.

9

Liz would be the worst kind of asshole if she evicted Beth. The crack in Beth's voice as she'd thanked Liz for her mediocre apology cut through everything; hopefully she could make these plans work. She deliberately ignored the little voice in the back of her head that screamed Petunia's name. This wasn't the same at all.

"Does that mean we are friends again?" She covered up the rough emotion in her voice with a cough.

"Shit, Liz. We aren't bloody teenagers. Life is a little more complicated than that." Beth's laugh made Liz's skin feel tighter.

"I've never been in this situation before. It's a bit confusing."

"Welcome to the club. I didn't appreciate being made aware that my new landlady was my online friend."

"If I'd known, I wouldn't have bought the building."

"I don't believe that."

Liz gasped at Beth's assertion.

"And more than that, I think you are glad it was you that bought my building, because you…"

As much as she didn't want to admit it… "You are right. I would hate for you to have to deal with another landlady. I want to look after my friend. I'm sorry about the power difference that this places between us. I truly am. I'm torn between it being a natural part of life and not wanting it to affect our friendship."

"It's a little late for that." Beth shook her head. "The friendship is already affected. To be honest, it's not even about the building. Once an online friendship moves into real life, it changes, no matter the reason. Online, we had a friendship that revolved around the plant parents. Both of us only told selected parts of our life. Now we've seen each other, you know I have a prosthetic leg, I know you are a bit older than me and much, much wealthier."

"You make my money sound like an insult."

"No. It's just reality. Seraph's makes enough money to keep it going and to pay me a living wage. It's never going to create the type of income I'd need to buy my own building."

"But…"

Beth held up her hand. "Trust me. When the building was first listed for sale, I did the sums. It was out of reach and that's okay. Of course I'd love to be my own landlady, but not if I can't afford it. I'm not going to spend my life struggling to pay a huge sum to a bank when I can pay an affordable sum to a landlady."

"I could help you put together a plan if you want."

"A plan for what?"

"Maybe owning the building for Seraph's is out of reach, but you could probably afford a small apartment for yourself. I assume you live alone." Liz wanted to help and even as she spoke, she recognised the same desire that had caused so much trouble with Petunia. She held her breath, waiting to see what Beth would say, and knowing that if she was too keen, Liz would have to call it a red flag and walk away. But Beth shrugged casually.

"You see what I mean about being online friends and then meeting in real life. Being social online can really help when in tough times, but it's always going to have a sense of disconnection because of the selective way of communication on there."

"What do you mean?" Liz asked. She didn't think she'd held herself back in their DM chats.

"From all the things we've chatted about online, I assumed you were single, but I didn't know for sure."

Liz raised her eyebrows, prickling at the suggestion she had lied to Beth. "People lie about that in real life too. Catfishing isn't just an online phenomenon."

"No. The old 'she told me she was separated/getting a divorce/just working out somewhere to live' problem."

"People are greedy."

Beth cackled. "Says the fucking property investor. Yes, people are greedy."

"Is that how you see me?" Liz blinked against the heat behind her eyes. *What the hell?* Obviously Beth didn't believe anything Liz had said in their online chats.

"Mmm, yes and no. Obviously I've seen how you can change your stance when given new information, but I don't necessarily like that I feel I had to tell you an emotional sob story to get you to see my point of view."

"Oh." Liz blinked rapidly. "Are you always this insightful?"

"Nah. I save that for you." Beth winked. Liz gulped. She really needed to change the subject to something less intense, otherwise she might just crawl over the table and kiss Beth.

What?

She never had the urge to do that for anyone, and certainly not so early in a friendship. Her heart beat so loudly that surely everyone in this tiny sushi shop could hear it.

"You're right, you know," she cleared her throat. "Um, about online interactions and assumptions. When I first met you in the Plant Parent group, I thought you must be a school teacher, or in HR, or some other type of job that meant you had to be good at keeping people's emotions in check."

"A teacher." Beth looked delighted by that assessment of herself. She giggled and the sound vibrated in Liz's chest, a direct jolt of energy into her heart. "I'd be a terrible teacher. We'd just listen to music all day and dance around the room."

"I can imagine that." Liz smiled. "Come on, what did you think of me?"

"Of you, or what job did I assume you did?"

"The latter, please."

"The latter? How fucking posh is that!"

"Hush." Liz's face heated.

"To be honest, I never thought about what job you might do outside the group. When you joined, it was in the rush of people who'd been thrown into pandemic lockdowns and wanted to bring outside indoors to help them cope."

Liz nodded. "Yes, that was my reasoning too. I am a keen rambler and like to spend my weekends walking some of the many paths around the country."

"Rambler?"

"It's like hiking. Our rambling group also helps maintain the different walking paths throughout the country."

"Does that maintenance include accessibility?"

Liz understood what Beth was hinting at and the answer wasn't perfect. "Mostly. I mean, all the walks are rated by difficulty, and many are wheelchair accessible."

"Okay. So I can just jump on their website and find out which ones I can do?"

Liz considered this for a moment. "I imagine you can do a lot more than most people assume, although you did say that you can't dance anymore?"

"I can dance. Just not burlesque."

"Oh?"

Beth shook her head, not wanting to explain the ableism in burlesque. She loved the power that came with exposing her body to an audience on her own terms. "It's complicated."

"Lots of things are."

"Yes." Take her emotional response to Liz for instance… It was so nice to have come to an arrangement over her club and get back to their old banter. She probably should go before the delicate arrangement became undone. "I'd better go. The sushi here is great. I need to be getting back to the club to get ready for this evening." They hadn't even ordered, and now Beth's stomach rumbled. She'd grab a couple of rolls to go on the way out.

"Are you open on Thursdays?"

"Every evening except Monday. Thursdays is our open dance night."

Liz frowned. "What does that entail?"

"We run dance classes during the day, and on Thursdays we open up the stage for anyone to dance. Often it's people from our dance classes who want to have a turn at dancing in front of an audience. Sometimes we get random people who want to dance without any training, which can be interesting, and sometimes we get dancers who want a paid gig with us who use it as an audition."

"Oh, that sounds like you'd get a wide range of things happening."

Beth chuckled. "Yeah, it can get a bit wild at times. We don't charge for entry on a Thursday because patrons are taking a chance on what they might see."

"You usually charge an entry fee?"

"Only on Friday, Saturday, and Sunday nights, because people are paying to see the best burlesque dancers in London. The price depends on who is dancing; we have our regulars, and we also showcase dancers from around the world sometimes. It was a lot more, you know, before." Beth missed hosting the championship events, from the local London one, to the nationals, and one memorable year, they'd hosted the World Championships with the best dancers from around the globe. The National Championships hadn't even been held for the last two years.

"I know what you mean. I'm not sure we'll ever go back to the way things were before."

Beth didn't want to dwell on it. "From a business point of view, we used to do great trade with tourists, and we could repeat our dancers a lot more often as we didn't have as many regulars. It's been a challenge for Charlie to ensure the show stays fresh every night, and we've had to reduce the door price because it's become a place where people come to meet and chat, rather than for the show. With a strong tourism trade, we could put on the same show for weeks on end before it became stale."

"Vaccines must be helping with that?"

Beth nodded. "It's slowly getting there, isn't it? We use our Saturday show as a tourist showcase now; it's a lot more expensive so we tend to only get one-off visitors and Ben and Reiko have done a great job in marketing those nights to Londoners too."

"It sounds like a complicated business model."

"All hospitality needs to constantly change to stay relevant." Beth couldn't help throw a little dig at Liz. "We recently renovated the whole place with the help of a government grant designed to get hospitality venues back on track after the lockdowns."

"Another reason not to knock the place down for a while."

"Yeah." Why wasn't it satisfying when Liz understood her backhanders? Probably because she was being a poor friend by throwing them at her, but she wasn't going to trust Liz immediately. She needed more evidence of solid plans before she truly believed that Liz wanted to help keep Seraph's as it was. She stood up.

"I'd better get going." She had work to do. Tonight was the first evening for Jonti's pop-up restaurant and it combined with one of Charlie's dance classes wanting to take over the whole evening with a 1930s themed burlesque night. There would be feathers and garters a plenty tonight.

"I'll come by as soon as I have news on next door."

"Okay. I guess I'll see you then."

"Or online before that?"

"Sure." Beth tucked her phone into the inside pocket of her leather jacket and zipped it up as she walked up to the front desk. She bought a couple of sushi rolls to go; salmon and avocado, and a teriyaki chicken one. Leaving Liz behind was becoming a satisfying habit.

10

_____

"Gin and Tonic, please," Liz said. The red-haired bartender mixed her drink efficiently and passed it to her. She tapped her card to pay, then wandered to a table in the corner. From here, she could watch the bar and the stage and most of the room.

Two weeks had passed since she'd had lunch with Beth and she'd been busy. She'd waited until she had a signed contract with the vendor of the property next door before coming here to give Beth the good news. She'd wanted to tell Beth as soon as they'd agreed to sell but had waited until everything was signed, and she'd paid the deposit first. Neither party could pull out of the deal now without a financial penalty. Holding this news inside had been more difficult than she'd imagined. It would still be a month or two before the sale was completed with all the paperwork and finances settled, and then she could start the next stage of the process. Liz had already started looking into the architects she wanted to tender for the job and would use the settlement period to put together the tender documents. Now the project was bigger and more complex, the planning would take more than the usual eight weeks she'd originally allocated. In hindsight, eight weeks had been hugely optimistic.

During the last two weeks, she'd chatted to Beth online in the Plant Parent group a few times. It'd been awkward, stilted, although occasionally either of them would forget about their real world tensions and would slip back into their old communication style. In those wonderful moments, Liz would remember the way Beth had swung her leg over her motorbike and raced off into traffic. What was the saying? The image lived rent free in her head. Sometimes she felt too old for all the internet and meme language; the internet had been brand new when she was a teen and she belonged to the generation who straddled the pre- and post-internet worlds. Kids these days had no idea of the agony of waiting for dial-up with that dreadful screeching sound, and then having her parents kick her off because they needed to use the phone. The download speeds of websites now were so incredible compared to those early days.

She nursed her Gin and Tonic as she waited for Beth to appear. Yes, she could have told her online, but she wanted to deliver the news in person. It was weird though. She didn't have Beth's mobile number. The only way she had for contacting her was through the Plant Parent website. She really ought to change that. She didn't want to ask her lawyers for Beth's contact details because it felt like a breach of confidentiality to use that route when all she had to do was ask through a communication channel they already had together. Was it weird to just turn up at her work?

Doubt settled in as a companion to her empty table.

Maybe she should go, and just send Beth a message online. She could ask for her phone number and meet up for lunch again. Damn it, she was a nearly fifty-year-old business woman. She shouldn't be so bloody nervous. With a swallow, she realised why. She wanted to make Beth smile, to please her, and maybe hopefully kiss her.

Did she really?

She sipped her gin again, trying to focus on the flavours to ground her back into the real world.

"Hello. Fancy seeing you here."

Liz opened her eyes, suddenly unsure when she'd closed them. "Hi. I have some news."

"That sounds ominous."

"It's not. I promise. I have good news." Liz felt like a giddy teenager around Beth.

"Okay?"

"The neighbours agreed to sell to me."

"Great."

Liz frowned. "You don't sound thrilled."

"In one week, I'm being evicted."

"Now you can stay." Liz gulped. She hadn't realised the timing had been so tight. "I have a proper contract for you, one that outlines all the terms and conditions that we both need to fulfil. It guarantees that you'll stay in this building until the one next door is built, and that you'll have input into the design and construction stages for next door so you can move in when you are satisfied with it."

"And the pitfalls?"

"I thought you'd be pleased."

Beth ran her hand through her short hair and her fringe

flopped back over her forehead. "I am." She didn't sound excited, she sounded exhausted.

"Are you okay?"

"Yeah, just been working hard, that's all." Oh, Beth's quietness likely wasn't to do with Liz at all. What a relief.

"Are you able to get some rest?"

"Sure."

"Are you dismissing me? I'm your friend, Beth."

Beth sighed. "I'm not dismissing you. The club has been busy lately and with the new pop-up restaurant opening, there's been a lot more work. I haven't really got the head space to focus on you."

"I'm sorry. I wondered if it might be weird to turn up while you were working, but I didn't know how else to contact you."

"We literally talked online yesterday."

"I'd rather do business in person. Can I have your phone number? We could meet up sometime."

Beth pulled her phone from the back pocket of her jeans and thumbed it open. She handed it over and Liz added her contact details, then sent herself a text so she'd have Beth's number too.

"Thanks."

"No problem. Enjoy the show. And thanks. It is good news." Beth took her phone and walked away with the distinctive sway in her hips due to her slightly uneven gait. It added to her appeal for Liz, and she wasn't sure quite how to process that information. She didn't want to mention it or even think it because wasn't it a bit creepy to notice? Beth could hardly change that she wore a prosthetic limb, and as much as she'd tried to blame herself for the car accident, it was just an accident. Liz instinctively knew Beth wouldn't want to be treated any differently because of it.

She grabbed her phone and read her own awkward text to herself from Beth's phone before adding her contact information. Liz flicked through her emails, finding nothing important except the reminder from Sreesha that they'd agreed to ramble together on Sunday. It would be so good to be getting back out into nature with the cold autumn wind on her cheeks and the trees turning into beautiful colours, scattering the ground with golds, oranges, and yellows.

B y the time the show ended, Liz was a little tipsy. She'd ended up grabbing the cheese platter and had drunk another two gins—two too many. She needed some water, so she wandered up to the bar and waited her turn before ordering. Beth served her with a faint smile.

"Thanks. Great show tonight." Liz didn't really get the appeal of burlesque. Yes, the dancers were athletic, and the costumes were aesthetically pleasing but she didn't find it sexy. Judging by the comments from many of the audience, she was unique in that view. Again. Well, whatever, she was old enough now that she didn't need to compare herself to others. Plenty of people were on the demisexual or ace spectrum and it was perfectly valid to be herself.

"Can you stick around for a while? I can talk after we close up."

"Absolutely." Liz hadn't expected that, and she started to say more but Beth had already moved on to serve the next person.

The song ended and a little bell rang. "We are legally

obliged to remind everyone that closing time is in half an hour." The MC strutted back and forth across the front of the stage, wearing only a g-string and bra, as she spoke. "I can see that everyone is having a great time, and it is unfortunate that our licence means we have to close at 1am. Please don't harass our bar staff. If you don't like having to leave us—and I don't blame you for that—you can write an email to the local council to get the zoning laws changed. I'm The Gloved Gatsby and you've all been a wonderful audience tonight." The speech came with a few groans from people beside her at the bar, although most people were already packing up and leaving. At least she knew she'd only have to sit here for another half hour before she was able to chat to Beth. No wonder Beth looked exhausted. Did she do these hours every night?

The time passed quickly. Between sipping her water and people watching, and a visit to the rest rooms, before she knew it, the bar was empty and only the staff walked around the room, efficiently tidying up.

"Everyone, gather over here for a bit." Beth's voice rang out across the room, and people arrived from all over the place. Dancers emerged from back stage in various states of dress, some of them in casual wear, others with dressing gowns over their costumes. A tall thin Black man with glasses jumped off the front of the stage, and the Pacific Islander security guard locked the front doors before walking towards the bar. A petite Asian woman, the one who'd picked up all the discarded costumes all night, leaned against one of the dancers, a lean white woman with a short bob cut.

"Everyone. This is Liz. She's our new landlady."

The room exploded into an antagonistic noise.

"Hush now. I have some good news. We aren't being thrown out anymore." Beth smirked and shot Liz a lengthy look as if she'd known exactly what the reaction would be. "Liz, if you would explain?"

Gosh, where to start? This was a tough crowd who obviously adored Beth and would defend her. She must be an incredible boss to garner such loyalty.

"Hold on, where is Jonti?" The red-haired bartender asked. "I'll get him." She darted through the double doors behind the bar and Liz breathed out slowly. This would give her a moment to gather her thoughts. Soon enough, the pair joined the group and Beth coughed.

Liz drew in a deep breath. Time to face her audience. "When this building was listed for sale, I realised that it was an excellent commercial opportunity. The zoning allows for new construction up to five storeys."

"Gentrification is evil." Someone called out and a couple of people cackled.

"I hardly think that applies here. Obviously, I made my initial plans before I met Beth and saw her determination to save her club. Once I understood the situation, Beth and I discussed options on how we could both achieve our goals." Liz took in an unsteady breath, but no one said anything snide. "To aid in that, I've also purchased the two neighbouring buildings, and before you say anything, this is simply business. There will be a two stage development; I'll demolish the two neighbouring buildings and build a new apartment block. Beth has agreed to work with the architect to design the entire ground floor of the new building as a new location for Seraph's Burlesque Club, and once this is done, the club will move into the new facility next door, and this building will be demolished as part of phase two."

"So, we get to stay?" The bartender asked.

"Yes. Not just that, but you will get input into the new construction and will end up with a high spec club that fits all your needs."

"We just need to live next to a construction site for how long?"

"Best case a year, worst case scenario, maybe three years. It's the best of all the options," Liz said. "Construction will be during the day, and since the club is mostly open in the evenings, there isn't going to be construction noise while you are open." Liz could say that with certainty even though she hadn't submitted any plans to the council yet.

"As long as it doesn't interfere with business, then I'm sure that's fine," Beth said.

"Change is difficult for everyone." Liz went for a soft tone, but given the way most people stared at her, she'd missed the mark.

"Yeah, except you. Without you, we wouldn't even have this conversation." Someone called out.

Liz focused on keeping a poker expression. "True. You might have less than a week left on your lease if someone else had bought this building. When a commercial building is offered for sale, the tenants often have little say in what comes next. It's only because I have come to admire Beth and her business acumen that we've been able to negotiate a better outcome for the club."

"I don't think that makes you sound as heroic as you'd like."

"I hate how rich people just come in and make decisions that we all have to just live with."

"Not all rich people, look at Reiko."

"I'm more of an outlier. You are right to be cautious with your trust." The loud discussion among a couple of the people in the group shouldn't hit Liz in the throat like this. She was proud of her construction projects and her commercial developments; in the long run, they made the city more financially accessible for more people by increasing the amount of housing options.

"Business isn't personal. It's a matter of negotiation and I feel this deal is a good one for both myself and Seraph's. Beth?" Liz asked.

"Given the choice of having to move elsewhere and being involved in a redevelopment that allows us to move next door, I'd take next door. How about we all celebrate that we don't have to move?" Beth said. "I want everyone to put together a wish list of all the things you'd want in the new building."

"What about us?" The bartender asked quietly.

"Steph and Walter rent one of the apartments above the club." Beth nodded in the direction of both the red-haired bartender—Steph—and the security guy—Walter. Now Liz could stop calling them by descriptions.

"That arrangement can continue in the new building."

"At the same price?" Beth asked, and Liz almost grinned at the way Beth had deliberately pushed her to agree in public. Clever.

"Yes." Initially at least, but Liz was wise enough to keep her mouth shut on any potential changes. She wasn't about to hike up the price as soon as everyone was settled, but now she'd seen the amount Beth paid to rent her building, it was no wonder the old owner wanted to sell. The return on investment rate must have been tiny for the previous owner since Beth paid much less than current market rate. If Liz had to bet, the rents hadn't been increased for a decade. No wonder Beth was keen to stay because it would be virtually impossible to rent a similar sized space for that rate anywhere in London. Liz had crunched her own numbers and she could keep Beth's rent the same by making a profit on the rest of her new building though the rent or sale of the new apartments.

"Good night everyone. Now you know the latest news. Seraph's isn't going anywhere." Beth waved her arm at the door and everyone started to wander off, although a few people lingered to whisper comments to Beth who nodded solemnly at each one.

11

_____

Beth couldn't quite reconcile the abrupt business version of Liz with her online friend. Once everyone had left and they stood alone in the empty bar, Liz let out a long sigh, one that Beth felt too. She was so fucking tired after running around for two weeks with Jonti's pop- up restaurant. It was going great, they'd made a lot more money than they'd expected, and their socials had gone wild with joy over his menu. But damn, it took so much energy to get it happening as well as all the usual club business.

"That went well?" Liz asked, hesitantly.

"None of them have any choice in the matter. They just want to keep their jobs secure." Beth didn't have the energy to deal with Liz's sudden doubts.

"And we've achieved that, so what is the problem?"

"It's hard to explain. Look, it's late, can we sort this out another time?" Beth stifled a yawn.

"Of course. Here take the contracts and read them over when you have time, then call me and we can go through any questions you have." Liz opened her briefcase and pulled out... a book? No, just a giant lump of papers bound together into a book.

"Seriously?"

"What?"

"That's the contract you want me to sign? How can you make it so complex?" Beth was way too tired for this. "You know what... Whatever. Hand it over. I need to sleep." She held out her hand and Liz gave her the fucking pile of paper. She tossed it on a table.

"You can't leave it there."

"Why not, Liz? Why the fuck not? No one else is going to read it."

Liz just stared at her. "You look exhausted. Let me help you."

"Now you want to help?" Beth was being rude but damn, she just wanted to take off her shoes and leg, lie down, and close her eyes.

"Yes. I've wanted to help ever since I knew this was your club."

"Funny way of showing it, but whatever." Beth could do with the help. "You carry the fucking bible of law. Wait there." She walked around the club, doing her usual routine, making sure everything was turned either off or on; the fridges were on, the oven was off, turning off the lights in the kitchen, behind the stage, and every other room back-stage, and finally checking that the doors were locked. Every night, she went through the exact same routine, walking the same pathway around the whole building, making sure everything was bedded down for the night and following morning. Once she'd checked the front door—even though Walter would have locked it already—she switched off the main lights in the club, leaving only a small light at the edge of the bar on.

"Come on then." She waved towards the hallway that led to the stairs for the upstairs apartments. Once Liz had followed her through, she locked the door that separated the club from the apartments, then made her way to her flat. She unlocked her own door, then took off her shoes.

"Are you going to stay?"

"Um." Liz cleared her throat. "Do you want me to?"

"Yes. I'm too fucking tired to let you out again." Just the thought of walking back down the stairs, letting Liz out, then locking up again, before hauling her tired arse upstairs again was too much. Her stump ached at the thought of it.

Liz chuckled. "That's not exactly an enthusiastic invitation."

"Whatever."

"I'll stay. Let me be your friend." Liz placed the stupid tome of a contract on a side table and put her briefcase on the floor beside it. Beth startled at the domesticity in that little motion. She would not get emotional at the idea of having a friend in her house. The prickle of heat behind her eyes had to be pure tiredness, nothing else. It wasn't like Liz was the first woman she'd brought home here. Living above the club meant it was much more convenient to bring her hook ups here, rather than go to wherever they lived. Since starting Seraph's, Beth had taken many people to bed, although none of them were her landlady and friend.

"Okay. I'm going to bed." She forced her body through her pre-bed routine, and when she lay down, and dragged the covers over her, she was asleep almost before her head hit the pillow.

. . .

Beth was starving when she woke up. The sun streamed inside the tiny window in her bedroom, so it must be about midday by now. She rolled over to check her phone. No batteries. Damn it. She reached further and plugged it in. The bed was warmer than usual and it made a funny breathing noise. What the fuck? Surely she hadn't brought someone home last night, she'd been far too tired for any shenanigans. She turned her head.

"Liz?" A vague memory of last night floated past. Had she really asked Liz to stay? Well, no. She'd kind of told her to stay. The randomness of it caught in her throat as an almost giggle. Liz didn't seem to notice; she lay on her back, staring at the phone in her hands.

"What are you doing?"

"Reading a book."

"Um, no. What are you doing in my bed? Did we...?" Beth hadn't exactly invited her into her bed last night, that much she was sure of, but she'd been so exhausted and hadn't fucked anyone for a while, so there was some chance of action.

Liz's cheeks flushed and she put her phone down. "No. You were very tired last night. I helped you come home and go to bed, and then I was tired too. You don't have a couch, and I'm too damned old to sleep on the floor, so I hope you don't mind."

"I don't mind."

"Why don't you have a couch?"

Beth laughed. "That's your question?"

"Yes."

"There is only one of me. A chair will suffice, and a couch would take up too much room. I'd rather have space for plants."

"Now that I understand." Liz grinned. "Your collection is incredible."

"Thanks. It was really Jewel's thing, and when she died, I kept them alive for her. It took a while to understand why she liked them so much; at first I resented that she left me with them. I'd rather have her than some bloody plants…"

"Oh." Liz rolled slightly, close enough that Beth could feel her breath on her cheek.

"I've grown to like them. I wouldn't have kept them for thirteen years if I wasn't getting something more out of it than dealing with grief. The Plant Parent group helped too. When I first joined I was struggling to keep them alive and I got more than just advice. I discovered people who understood my situation, and I made friends." Beth hadn't really articulated this to anyone before. There was something about Liz's patient expression that made her want to talk.

"It's important to have friends."

"And extra important not to fuck them over by buying the building they rent and threatening to throw them out." Beth winked to let Liz know she was jesting. She was—mostly—over the sense of betrayal she'd initially felt because Liz had worked so hard to try and fix things.

"Hey."

"I'm joking." Beth grinned. "I can't believe you bought the building next door to try and make amends. It's one hell of a grand gesture."

A frown flickered across Liz's brow and her cheeks flushed slightly pink. "Was it too much?"

"No. Look, I might have said a few things when I first found out that my new landlady was also my online friend —" Beth hadn't been kind and it wasn't fair since Liz had worked hard to make amends.

"Don't."

"What?"

"It's fine. I deserved everything you said. I hold the cards here. I'm the one who has the financial power, and I should be the one who makes amends. Don't you dare feel bad for advocating for yourself."

"Okay."

"I'm really looking forward to planning this project with you."

"With me?" Beth knew that technically they'd agreed that Beth would have some say in the new building and the new layout for Seraph's, but she had assumed her involvement would be fairly distant.

"Yes. I've been thinking about it a lot over the last couple of weeks, and—" Liz paused for a couple of breaths and Beth waited. "—please don't take this the wrong way. I don't think of you as a charity."

"Um, thanks?"

"Seriously though. This isn't the first time I've worked with a business who rents a building I own."

"But?" Beth was sure she heard that word—but—in the background of whatever Liz was thinking.

Liz sat up. "It's weird having this conversation while lying in bed with you. Are you okay with that?"

"Sure. I'm comfortable having you in my bed. Now stop procrastinating and just say it."

"This is the first time I've worked with a tenant who was

already my friend before we started the process, and I'm a bit lost because I want to value our friendship first and foremost..."

"But?"

"Architecture can be a stressful process and I don't want to stress our friendship."

Beth found all this second guessing frustrating. She forced her jaw to relax, obviously it mattered to Liz to work through everything like this. "I'm pretty sure we've already done the stressful part."

Liz shook her head and sighed. "Yes and no. This is just the start of it and I'm really unaccustomed to working with someone else."

"Look." Beth sat up beside Liz. She instinctively brushed her fingers along Liz's jaw, and Liz turned to face her. "If we both commit to listening to each other then it'll be fine." Beth wanted to kiss Liz, which made no sense, given the current discussion and their history, but it also made complete sense because she was here, in her bed, talking about how she could be a better friend to Beth. And it'd been an age since Beth had fucked someone, so the proximity to a sexy body was making her a bit horny. A lot horny. Liz was bloody lovely with her pink smudged cheeks and her sparkling eyes.

"I can work with that, provided..."

"Always with the legal sub clauses." Beth didn't roll her eyes but it was a close thing.

"Are you determined to think the worst of me? No, don't answer that. I was going to say that I might need help with listening. It's not my strongest suit; I've been independent for a long time."

Beth tried not to grin. "What a pair we are. I'm also used to only having to answer to myself. This is going to be an interesting few months."

"Interesting. The way you say that is—"

"Interesting?" Beth laughed and Liz joined in. From there it was the most natural thing in the world to lean closer and brush a soft kiss against her lips. The perfection of Liz's lips against her own meant that it took her a few seconds to realise that Liz hadn't moved; in fact, her eyes darted back and forth as if she were incredibly uncomfortable. Beth pulled her face away quickly.

"I'm sorry."

"Don't be sorry. You surprised me, that's all."

"Does that mean you want more kisses?"

"Maybe." Well, it wasn't a no, even if it was a bit confusing. They were in bed together, and Beth had been sure she'd felt a chemistry between them.

"Do you think we have chemistry?"

Liz frowned. "Maybe. Look, this is awkward. I'm demisexual, so—"

"Oh." Beth understood. "I'm sorry. Take all the time you need. I can wait."

"Thanks."

"And hey—" Beth touched Liz on the hand, then jerked it away again. "It's not awkward. I hope I haven't been too overtly allosexual around you." Beth was like the majority of people, not needing an emotional connection with someone to have sex with them. She was a fan of hate fucking as much as any other type of fucking—it was an excellent way to release energy. One thing about running a burlesque club was meeting people all across different sexual and gender spectrums and she'd taken the time to learn, and keep learning, all the terminology that people liked to use to describe themselves. Burlesque was a wonderful way for people to express themselves and the club was an open and safe environment for people. She hoped she hadn't overstepped too much with Liz.

"No, you've been fine. I mean, we've had a whole friendship to resolve first. The fact that I'm in your bed and you've respected my boundaries means a lot to me." Liz breathed in deeply, and Beth waited because it felt like Liz had more to say. "Most people don't really get it. It's fair, I suppose, I don't understand how people can just have sex without emotional connection."

"It's just bodies. A physical release enjoyed with someone else."

"Yeah. Not for me."

"It's okay. Everyone has their own way of being and that's perfectly valid." Beth didn't want to push for more information. "There's one thing I should clarify."

Liz raised her eyebrows.

"I am physically attracted to you, and I wouldn't be averse to kisses if or when you are ready."

"Thank you."

Beth's stomach grumbled. "Shit. Sorry." She didn't really need her stomach to jump into this conversation just yet because she wanted to understand Liz a bit more. From what she'd said so far, Liz would tell her when she was ready, so it was better if she focused on eating now and just let Liz talk when she wanted. "Let me make you some food."

"That sounds good."

Beth grabbed her leg and put it on, then stood up and

walked to her small kitchen. She didn't have anything too fancy for breakfast; normally she'd just make herself a sandwich at this time of day. Well, she could make a toasted sandwich as a special treat instead.

"Are you warm enough?"

"What?"

"You aren't wearing very many clothes."

Beth wore underwear and a loose shirt. "I'm fine. I can put more clothes on if you want."

"No. I'm demisexual, not a prude." Liz grinned and Beth smiled back.

"Okay. Yeah, I'm warm enough. This flat is well insulated and I tend to run hot anyway." Beth pulled out the toasted sandwich press and gathered some ingredients.

"Thanks for doing this." Liz stood beside the kitchen bench and flicked open the giant contract. "Did you know we have the same name?"

"Excuse me?"

"Elizabeth."

Beth hadn't used her full name in years. There were very few places where it was written down. One of those was her rental agreement for the building. "Liz as a nickname for Elizabeth. Nice. I take it that's why your handle is NotTheQueen?"

"Says QueenB."

"It used to be my burlesque name. Queen Bee; like the insect, and obviously a pun with my name."

Liz chuckled and Beth quickly made them both a sandwich. This domesticity with someone else was lovely; it'd been a lifetime since she'd done this, and she missed it. She missed the simplicity of caring for someone else's basic needs through food. She'd always done the cooking because Jewel worked long hours as an engineer. Cooking for just herself wasn't quite the same. It was more about sustenance than provision, and Beth tended just to throw a salad together or have a sandwich for dinner rather than bother to cook a whole meal. How nice would it be to have someone to cook for again? Patience. If she waited, maybe the chemistry between her and Liz would grow. Or it would fade. Either way, this time wasn't wasted. She could take a chance on Liz —her friend who'd just bought a fucking building to keep their friendship intact—and just see where it all went.

12

It took a few weeks to finally get an appointment with Liz's preferred architect, Morgan Adlem. Now that she was building two matching buildings, she wanted something more striking than her original idea to reuse plans she'd built before. Liz should be focusing on business and not the way Beth had kissed her in bed and her reaction afterwards, which had been so sweet and understanding. Liz had mused on it—a little obsessively—since then, but she still didn't know what she might do about it.

Over the years, she'd had a lot of different reactions from people when she told them she was demisexual, or even just that she needed some time to form an emotional connection first. Not too many knew the word—which was fine—and honestly, she knew from the way people responded whether it would be worth persisting with the friendship. Beth's reaction had been perfect. She'd understood, apologised for going too fast, and had given her space.

They'd chatted and texted over the last two weeks with

each comment reminding Liz of the kiss. She might just want another one.

"Liz. It's so good to see you." Beth must have ridden her bike here as she wore the same leather jacket, paired with a shimmering silver threaded v-neck t-shirt that made her cleavage look amazing. Oh. Liz barely ever noticed people's bodies apart from general aesthetics; the kiss and all the contemplation must have been slowly forming connections.

"Likewise."

"This place is pretty fancy."

"Yes. I like it." Liz loved buildings like this. "I particularly love the way they have perfectly blended a three-hundred-year-old heritage building with a modern façade. It's a stunning piece of restoration with an innovative connection between old and new."

"You really do like it."

Liz shrugged, slightly uncomfortable at having been so enthusiastic. "Yes. It's clever business too. Adlem and Smithson have showcased their architectural abilities with this restoration, and if they can pull off a negotiation like this with English Heritage, then they will be able to manage my expectations."

Beth grinned. "Your expectations? What exactly are they?"

"I chose Adlem and Smithson because they responded to my tender documents with an acceptable ballpark price and a design that pulled in the elements I wanted." Liz tried not to stare too hard at Beth's expression. "I know I sound like a hard-hearted business person…"

"You don't. You sound passionate about architecture."

Liz's cheeks heated. "Thank you."

"Ms Adlem will see you now." The young man on reception opened a door for them, and they walked into a huge office with floor-to-ceiling glass window on one wall, and bookshelves lining two of the other walls.

"Ms Whitten? I'm Morgan Adlem and I'm so pleased you liked our proposal."

"Hi. Please call me Liz. This is Beth Zendeli." Liz wasn't sure how to introduce Beth, so she just ignored the need for a label. Tenant sounded weird in this context, although it was likely the most appropriate.

"Great to meet you, Beth. Do you want tea or coffee?"

"No thanks."

Liz shook her head too, and Morgan waved to a group of seats by the window.

"Let's go over the initial proposal, shall we? And then we can talk about the specific needs for the building."

"Excellent." Liz sat down and waited as Morgan spread out some drawings over a coffee table between them. The concept plans were the same as the one in the tender document and looked amazing with the green walls incorporated into the exterior cladding. Morgan talked through the plans and then asked if they had any questions.

"Yes. Is this the entrance for the club?" Beth pointed at the drawing.

"At this stage, we've kept the design deliberately vague as we'll need to understand the proposed usage of the building before we add in details like that."

"I mentioned in the tender documents that the building will need two main entrances," Liz said. "One for the apartments that will take up levels one through five, and one for the first floor facilities including Beth's club."

"Club?" Morgan's tone changed slightly and Liz stiffened. It wasn't unusual in this location for the ground floor of a building to be filled with commercial enterprises, especially in the entertainment space.

"My club will take up the majority of the ground floor."

Liz cleared her throat. "The design of the club will be up to Beth, hence her presence in this meeting today."

Morgan relaxed a little as she realised the working relationship between the two. "It's unusual to have a tenant involved in this phase."

"Yes, well, Beth's club currently exists in the building that will be phase two, and as part of the development process, we've agreed to build a new facility in phase one to reduce the disruption on the club."

"Unique, but I like it. Cooperative projects are my favourite type."

"What happens now?" Beth asked.

"I'd like to create a list of what you will need in the new club facility and if it's okay, I'd love to come and visit the current club to get a handle on the layout and what you'd like to improve in the new build."

"We are open every evening except Monday. And you should probably talk to Elle Denbigh-Yadav of D&Y Designs as she has the full set of plans for the club. We recently did a complete refit using one of the government grants available to hospitality businesses."

"She's very exclusive," Morgan sounded impressed and Liz made a mental note to do more research into D&Y Designs.

"Mate's rates." Beth winked. "Elle is a friend of mine, so we were able to work out a plan that worked within the restrictions of the grant. I'm sure she made no profit from working with us, however, she did get a lot of publicity from the work, so…"

"Ahh, using a friend as a loss leader for her business. That's clever business."

"A little hustle keeps everyone afloat."

"If it's good enough for the old guard of business, then we should be able to use the same techniques for our own advantages too." Morgan was pragmatic in the way she talked business, which Liz appreciated, but she really didn't like the way Beth leaned forward and grinned at her. Seeing Morgan flirt with Beth made her stomach churn a little with … jealousy? Huh. She barely heard the discussion between the two as they discussed the needs of the club because her head was spinning.

"How does that sound to you, Liz?" Morgan asked.

"If Beth is happy, I'm happy." She should just jump out the window now, as Morgan glanced between the two of them with speculation. "It's her club, not mine, so the design needs to fit the needs of the club. I'm just the landlady."

"And my client. My job is to ensure everyone is happy."

"As long as Beth's club works within the general struc-ture of the building and meets the necessary regulations, then I'm sure it's fine." She could hardly admit she had missed most of the discussion because she'd been thinking—again—about the way Beth's lips had brushed over hers. Her mouth felt dry, so she poured herself a glass of water from the jug on the table and gulped some down. It didn't really help.

She'd been kissed before, of course. She shouldn't be this

obsessive about a little kiss; a kiss that felt like she'd never been kissed before. She tried not to sigh as she admitted that it wasn't really the kiss, but the lovely way Beth had reacted afterwards with understanding and kindness. After the way Liz had treated Beth, she didn't really deserve that kindness.

"Once you visit Seraph's, Morgan, then you'll understand what I've been saying. I discussed some of these changes with Elle when we did the refit but they were too expensive."

"That's the beauty of starting from scratch. We can plan to have the ideal layout and can learn from the experience of the current facilities."

"I'd love to expand our dance classes too. One room works fine at the moment, but it does mean we can't schedule as many classes as we would like because of the hand over time between classes using the same room."

"Would it be good for the dance classes to have a separate entrance too?"

Beth shook her head. "Many of our dancers like to use the bar after their class, so we'd need to think carefully about that to ensure we still get the income from their after-class relaxation time."

Morgan made a note on her paper. "And the apartments above, Liz?"

"I'd like to have a blend of apartments and offices on the first floor above the club. Currently Beth and one of her employees rent the two apartments above the club, and that arrangement will need to continue." Liz wanted to set it up so Beth ended up owning her apartment, but after the mess with Petunia, she wasn't sure she wanted to open herself up to that possibility again. It only appealed because everything

Beth had said since they'd met in real life pointed to Beth saying no to such a proposal.

"Also if we move the club's office upstairs that frees up more space downstairs for public spaces and perhaps more dance class spaces," Morgan said.

"I like that idea," Beth said. Beth's little smile held Liz's attention, which was fortunate as Morgan tapped her pen and stared at Liz.

"In the tender, the floors above will be all residential apartments. Are you still happy with that?" Morgan asked.

"Yes. Ideally, I'd like to have a couple of levels of carparking underneath, however, that's going to depend on the constraints underground."

"I can get a services plan from the council and look at the potential archaeological issues."

Liz nodded. She'd done this several times previously, and London's long history tended to throw archaeological spanners in the works whenever people dug down and uncovered the layers of what had been there before. Car parking always helped sell apartments and the extra hassle of dealing with history would end up being worth it financially, unless they discovered something incredible like Roman ruins, or perhaps the skeleton of a king.

"What about the standard sizes of the apartments in this building? Where do you see the building fitting into the residential market?" Morgan asked.

It was an excellent question. "In this location, I think we'd want to go for middle of the market with mostly two and three bedroom apartments of an average size. Not too cramped and not too spacious, although we can obviously go a little more lux for the top floor."

"And with the green aspect, I'd love to include a roof top garden."

"Lovely. I would want that to be accessible to all apartments, not just the top floor ones." Too many buildings sold the penthouse apartments with the roof as exclusive space, but Liz liked to ensure all her apartments had access to outdoor relaxation spaces.

"Absolutely." Morgan made more notes in her book. The meeting finished soon after that with Morgan clarifying a few other details and they agreed to meet again in a few weeks with a draft plan for both buildings, which would ultimately mirror each other. Liz would need to find a new tenant for the phase two building, one that wouldn't compete with Beth, but would complement her business.

As they went down the lift to the street level, Liz checked her calendar. "Would you like to have some afternoon tea with me?"

Beth grinned. "Sure. Are you going to take me somewhere fancy?"

"If you like?"

"I'm joking. Tea sounds good. It's a little late for lunch and probably too early for a drink."

"A drink? It's not even three on a Wednesday."

Beth shrugged as if it didn't matter. "I have to work tonight so it's a moot point anyway. Tonight is Drag Trivia."

"Would it be alright if I came?"

"To trivia night, sure? I mean, I'll be working, so I can't hang out with you."

"I'll invite my friends again. We came once before when I'd first bought the building and I was doing research. It was brilliant fun."

"Helen and Reiko will be happy to hear that. Reiko makes the best questions."

"Yes, they were a good blend of easy and impossible. And Helen is a hilarious host. Come on, let's grab some tea in that little shop over the road. It looks cosy." Liz wanted to get out of the cool autumn breeze.

A fter they were seated and had ordered, Liz couldn't think of anything to say that hadn't already been said. Her current obsession with Beth's lips wasn't exactly something she wanted to discuss.

"The meeting went well," Beth said, filling the silence.

"Yes. I'm pleased with the progress today." Liz didn't need to rehash the meeting, although there were probably a few things they could talk about without Morgan flirting with Beth. "I wanted to talk about the second building."

"The one I'm in now?"

"Yes. Once both buildings are done, they'll be a mirror of each other, which means, the ground floor will suit a business of some sort."

"So rent it to someone." Beth shrugged.

"I would like your input into those decisions. After going through all this to save your business, I would hate to have a competitor move in next door."

Beth laughed. "There aren't a great number of people wanting to open burlesque clubs. There are only seven in all of London, although plenty of pubs hold burlesque events on occasion."

"I meant another club or pub or business who might compete with you for clients."

"I understand. I was kidding." Beth leaned back in her chair, a picture of relaxation and that's when Liz figured it out what was different.

"You've stopped arguing with me." And gone back to jokes. Their friendship had become more like their online friendship with less antagonism.

Beth laughed. "Don't tell me you miss it."

"No. Maybe a little bit. I mean—" Her cheeks were far too hot, and Liz wanted to duck under the table. She was bloody near fifty. It was ridiculous to blush at her age, or at any age, but her Scottish pale skin had always been a beacon for her emotions.

"Yeah?"

"I don't miss having you annoyed with me, and you look much nicer when you aren't exhausted."

"Nicer?" Beth grinned. "You know that it's not a woman's job to look nice for other people."

Liz spluttered. She was doomed to always upset Beth, wasn't she? "I didn't mean it like that. I just ... why is this so hard? I'm trying to compliment you."

Beth's laugh echoed around the small shop. "Thanks. It's good to know that I'm a better friend when I'm not being confrontational about your choice to upset my life."

"I thought you were over that?"

"I am. I'm teasing you. You can't have it both ways, Liz."

"I don't want that. This is better. It's just less energetic or something, I guess."

Beth sighed. "Rude energy isn't any better than calm energy or happy energy. I'd rather spend my time being productive than frustrated."

"I think I was just trying to figure out our friendship

and I …" Could she admit this? Yes. She'd started now. It would be odd to not finish. "I like the way you stand up for yourself."

"Okay? What is really bothering you?"

Liz frowned. "What do you mean?"

"You sound uncertain, and honestly, me being nice to you is hardly a problem."

"No, it's not."

"So what is the actual problem?"

Liz glared at Beth. "I don't want to talk about it." She couldn't tell Beth that she couldn't stop thinking about kissing her, and she might want to kiss her again. She felt like she had a schoolgirl crush and it was awful, in the nicest way.

Beth's eyebrows shot upwards, and she cackled. "Most people just change the subject if they don't want to discuss something. Instead, you've talked all around the edges of whatever the issue is; blaming me for being too nice lately, and now this…"

"Do you intend to be irritating on purpose?" Liz should never have invited Beth to afternoon tea. It was a mistake because all she wanted to do was admit her desires and she wasn't sure she was ready for that, just yet.

"Yes." Beth laughed louder. "Come on, you have to tell me now."

"I really don't."

"Fine. Let's talk about something different and I'll try and drag it out of you tonight."

Liz couldn't even glower at her. "I'd like to see you try."

Beth's smile lit up the whole room. "Excellent. Shall we order?"

13

Liz had been surprised when Beth had invited her home after the trivia night, and now she sat in Beth's bed, scrolling through emails while Beth slept beside her. Beth stirred, rolling over to fumble in the direction of her phone. She groaned a little as she stared at the screen, then rolled onto her back.

"Good morning."

"Um, hi."

"You don't remember inviting me here last night, do you?"

"Yeah, I do. Give me a sec." Beth's voice was a lower tone than usual, slightly husky. She rubbed her eyes, then sat up in bed. The blanket fell down around her waist, and her thin shirt didn't really hide her breasts.

"Are you cold?" Liz asked, attempting to disguise her interest with politeness. She was unable to look away from the tight buds of Beth's nipples showing through her sleeping shirt. She really needed to do something about this growing attraction she had to Beth; like kiss her again, because feeling like this was rare and special and it was worth dwelling on.

"No. I'm fine. Do you want to eat here, or go out?"

"Here is fine. I don't have a change of clothes, just what I wore last night." If they were going to be seen in public, Liz needed a shower and fresh clothes as well her own toothbrush.

"Okay." Beth swung out of the bed and stood on one leg. She bent over and put on her prosthetic with skilled hands. Obviously. Liz wanted to roll her eyes at herself. Of course Beth put on her prosthetic easily, she must do it every day, just as Liz knew how to tie her own shoelaces. Watching Beth move with elegance and competence overruled her own internal awkward monologue.

"I'd let you borrow my clothes, but your hips are broader than mine, so none of my pants are likely to fit you."

Beth knew her size? What did that mean? Liz swallowed. It just meant that Beth was observant, it didn't mean that Beth had measured her body or anything that might show that Beth was interested in Liz's shape.

"It's fine." Liz pinched her lips together before she said something silly like, next time.

"I have a new toothbrush in the bathroom if you want to use that, though. I can guarantee it's never been used by anyone before."

"Thank you." Liz ran her tongue over her slightly furry teeth. Being able to brush them would be fantastic.

"I'll just grab it." Beth left the room, leaving Liz alone in her bed. She got up and quickly threw on the clothes she'd worn last night. The skirt and blouse were far too dressy for sitting around and having breakfast in Beth's house, but they'd have to do as she had nothing else. She wandered into the kitchen, where Beth stood there in her sleeping shirt and underwear, making porridge. The smell of oats filled the room with a wholesomeness that made Liz want to belong here. A toothbrush, still in its packaging, sat on the kitchen bench. Liz picked it up and went to the bathroom to brush her teeth. When she returned with her mouth feeling a lot fresher, she sat on the stool beside the kitchen bench.

"Did you enjoy the trivia last night?"

Liz grinned. "We won again thanks to Sreesha."

"Sreesha?"

"One of my friends. He's a gun at trivia, he even won one of those tv trivia shows back in the early 2000s."

"A secret weapon." Beth grinned as she poured the porridge into two bowls. "Brown sugar? Cinnamon? Anything else?"

"Brown sugar and a tiny touch of salt for me. Thanks."

"I already added salt when I was cooking it. What kind of monster cooks porridge without a pinch of salt?"

"My parents."

"Oh no. That's one way to ruin a childhood!" Beth laughed.

"It's fine really. They were both doctors and thought that my diet already had enough salt in it, so I could do without it for breakfast."

"That's a fair point, I suppose. Boring, but fair."

Liz chuckled. "My parents weren't boring. They spent their lives working for an international medical charity. I was dragged around the world by them as a child, which was a great experience, although quite disruptive. I think that's why I prefer a quiet, boring life now."

"You aren't boring."

"I am. My job is passive, I like to walk around the countryside. When I travel, it's always to safe places that aren't challenging."

"You probably had enough challenges when you were a kid."

"Yes. I didn't mind it. I often had to entertain myself. That's how I began walking for something to do while my parents saved lives, and then when I was a teenager, I went to boarding school and only travelled with them during holidays."

"So they basically abandoned you for their work?"

Liz shook her head vigorously. She'd never felt abandoned by them. "No. That's not correct. They didn't abandon me. It wasn't like that. Their work was important."

"More important than their kid?"

"That's an unfair comment. They always made time for me, it's just that they were busy." Liz hadn't minded spending time alone. When she'd travelled with them, there were always local kids to play with and the nurses gave her little jobs to do to help out, and she had her school work and books, and the fresh air. It'd been fine. "I had plenty of opportunities that other kids didn't have. I can understand and mostly speak seven different languages and I've seen parts of the world that most people never get to."

"And yet you choose not to repeat those experiences."

Liz shrugged. "I'm not a doctor. I help people in other ways, ways that suit me." She was an introvert, someone who didn't have the same passions for being constantly surrounded by people like her parents.

"There's no need to get defensive about it. If you were

content as a child, that's a lot better than many other kids get." Beth started to eat her porridge which Liz took as a hint not to ask about her childhood. It didn't really matter as it was so long ago.

"I miss my parents. They loved me and they had so much passion and energy for their job. I was mostly content, and they inspired me to try and improve the world around me."

"Mostly?"

"If you are going to say they abandoned me again, you are wrong. I was just the odd one out in the family; they wanted to save the world and I liked … having my own space to exist in peace."

"An introvert to their extrovert?"

"Yes. Some people love going to disaster zones and helping. My parents loved the action and I guess, they liked feeling like heroes in a sense. I prefer to help from afar. Both options are okay."

Beth smiled. "See. That's not boring at all."

"The porridge is nice." Liz ate efficiently, glad to have something to do that prevented her from spilling more feelings. "It was a long time ago. I had a lucky childhood in many ways, it helped me understand the world and know my own privileges." She'd long ago dealt with her guilt around not being there with her parents when they'd died. As her therapist had said, it was their decision to go to Haiti and assist people and they knew the risks. She'd declined to go with them, just as she had on many other occasions. That they didn't return from this trip wasn't her fault.

It all sounded simple now, as simple as the warming flavour of the porridge with a touch of salt, a generous helping of brown sugar, and the sprinkle of cinnamon. Liz hadn't had porridge with cinnamon before but when Beth had suggested it, she had wanted to try it. See? She could be adventurous sometimes.

"Are you okay?" Beth asked.

"Yes. I haven't thought about some of this stuff for a while. Obviously when my parents died, the university suggested I go to counselling, and it helped. I've been alive for longer without them than I had with them."

"Ahh but childhood has a way of sticking with us even when we are old and apparently wise."

"Yes. Their death was ruled an Act of God by the life insurance company."

"Oh?"

"They were in Haiti working as doctors when a cyclone hit."

"Fuck." Beth summed it up pretty well.

"They died helping people. It strikes me as ironic that it was ruled an Act of God, when the whole reason they were there is because the world is unjust and unfair."

"And?"

"Well, if God was real, then the world would be more equal, wouldn't it?"

"Maybe. Depends on whose God is in charge, I suppose."

Liz laughed. After the porridge was done, she moved into the kitchen to help Beth clean up. Liz added detergent to the sink and washed the pot, both bowls, and their spoons, rinsing off the bubbles and placing them carefully to dry. Working alongside Beth increased Liz's awareness of her. Sexual attraction for her was always a little confusing; it'd be simple if it worked like a switch, but after nearly fifty years of listening to herself, Liz knew it was just a journey that she would go on and see what happened.

"It's a moot point. I've made my own life now. I have my work, my friends…" Liz almost said, 'you'.

"What is it like, being a property investor?"

"Are you asking me how I spend my time?"

"Yes. I'm curious. I run a business. I assume it's similar to that, doing accounts, and whatever."

Liz nodded. Talking about this was much easier ground than washing dishes without accidentally touching Beth's fingers as she took them off her to dry them. "Most of my properties are commercial, not residential, and tenants tend to be incredibly short term, or in it for the long haul, like yourself."

"I don't need reminding of our working relationship." Beth elbowed Liz and laughed.

"I deserved that. Okay, so the longer term tenants don't require much management apart from ensuring they pay regularly and sorting out any maintenance issues that arise. The most time consuming part is organising inspections and contracts for new tenants, and negotiating over how they will use the spaces and what changes they want to make."

Beth nodded. "Have I taken up too much time?"

"Never. Now that we are into the design phase, I'm really excited. I love the process of improving a location. Many of the buildings I buy are for the location, and I embark on a renovation or rebuild. Property is a long term prospect."

"It's such a different type of business to running a club which is all about staying fresh and keeping customers walking in the door."

"Yes. Slow and steady, that's my game."

Beth smiled. "You are lucky too. You don't have to deal with staff."

"Are your staff difficult?" They'd been pretty vocal several weeks ago when Liz had announced her purchase of next door.

"No. I have a really good core staff at Seraph's but hospitality staff tend to move about a lot. We always have a rotating set of temporary staff."

"During the lockdowns, I had to outsource a lot of the work."

"Was that difficult?"

"Yes." Liz heard the weight in her voice and she hoped Beth wouldn't ask anything more. "My lawyers were great in helping me set up contracts for everyone involved."

"Contracts?"

"I had a few problems with an assistant years ago—" She gritted her teeth. Why did she mention Petunia? Even in passing. It wasn't exactly something she was proud of. Her employee, turned girlfriend, who'd fooled everyone with her fake niceness until one day she had disappeared with a million dollars stolen from Liz.

"Ahh, now you are cautious." Beth emptied the sink and dried her hands. "And then I became a problem tenant who wouldn't shut up!"

Liz almost choked on her tongue. "You were not in the same league as Petunia's scam."

"Petunia? I'm sorry. What?"

"People can't help what names their parents give them." If it even was her real name… "She stole from me."

"Fuck. That's shit."

"Yes. She just vanished. The police have never found her or the money."

"I'm so sorry."

Liz shrugged. "Thanks. The thing that really hurt was that I could fall victim to a scam like that. She was so nice."

"I understand your reticence to deal with me when I first confronted you." Beth rubbed her hand on Liz's shoulder and Liz wanted to lean in and hug her. The worry about having another Petunia in her life was the only thing that stopped her.

"It happens. I've changed my processes and increased security since then." Liz sighed. "Enough about me. Now that we've resolved the major issues around the building, are you content?"

"I think so. I get to keep my club. My employees are like family to me, so it's satisfying to have a solution that allows us to continue in the same location. Starting over in a new place would've added a lot more stress."

"Good. I'm glad we have a pathway forward."

14

Beth nodded. What else could she do? They did have a pathway forward, and the revelation about Liz's thieving employee made it even more incredible that Liz would go to such lengths to find a solution that worked for them both. The generosity more than made up for the initial arguments. Liz dried her hands on a tea towel and hung it neatly.

"I really appreciate the amount of effort you've put into helping me. You didn't have to," Beth said.

"I did. As you pointed out several times, we are friends, and it would make me a terrible friend if I made a decision that hurt you."

"And bonus, this proposal means neither of us have to compromise."

Liz breathed out slowly. "Yes, or at least we don't have to compromise too much."

Beth scoffed. "Compromise isn't a dirty word."

"We've all had to make a lot of compromises since the pandemic began. Was it very tough for you?"

Trust Liz to ask one of the hardest questions.

"Yes, we had to change everything to keep this place going."

"What do you mean?"

"Before the pandemic, life was great. I had the club, I had lots of people around me. Every night we made people smile or laugh, and we created a space where anyone could come and have a good time without being harassed for who they are. It was brilliant, and when I missed..." Beth paused. She'd missed coming home to Jewel and being cared for, the companionship and having someone who wanted to be there for her. She wasn't going to mention any of that. "When I missed sex, there was always someone who could fulfil that need for me." Beth's throat tightened, suddenly all scratchy and dry. "Once we were locked down, I had far too much time to think without people to talk to. The Plant Parent group was fantastic for that, no matter the time of day or night, there was always someone to talk to, but I missed being hugged. I missed the small moments of connection with real people in the same room as me, the little touches, the connections, the flirting."

"I think it was a very tough time for extroverts. Several of my friends from rambling had similar difficulties."

"Yeah, and when we were finally able to open up again—"

Liz spun around and held up her palm. "Wait. Please don't tell me you were in favour of early opening?"

"No. What made you think that?"

"Many business owners thought the lockdowns were an overreaction. They wanted to keep things open to protect the economy. Many of my commercial tenants struggled to pay rent during the lockdowns with their staff working from home and the buildings staying empty."

"Quit reminded me that you are heartless landlady." Beth couldn't resist the jest, and she nudged Liz with her elbow. Liz smiled, shaking her head.

"I offered reduced rates, all the way down to nothing in some cases, for long term tenants who were consistent payers. It hurt, but not as much as COVID hurt everyone and I bounced back once people started wanting to go back to the office."

"Fair enough."

"I read a study that said that about twenty percent of people wanted to stay working from home, another twenty percent wanted to be full time in the office, and the rest wanted a blend."

"That's pretty interesting." Beth was in the get out the house and see people again group. "But to answer your question, early opening was nonsense, fuelled by greed, and such short term thinking. The economy is made of people, it literally only exists if people exist, and dead customers don't bring in any income."

"Yes."

"Even as hard as it was to be closed for so long, it was worth it to protect our current and future customers and everyone else. One of our dancers, Yolande, works as a nurse and I listened to her advice on the matter. Money isn't relevant if people are hurting, and well, you know how many people are grieving now because we didn't take the threat seriously enough." The number of people who'd died during the pandemic made Beth's head and heart ache; so much of it had been driven by selfishness.

"Thank you." Somehow Liz's eyes didn't glaze over at Beth's rant, instead gifting her with a heartfelt thanks.

Beth had been wrong; her assumption that Liz would be focused on dollars had been blown out of the water with her sensible, science-based reasoning.

"So you followed the advice of the medical experts?" Beth asked.

"Of course. My parents were doctors. It was easy to ask myself what they would have done, what they would want, and do that."

"Okay. That's sensible."

Liz grinned. "I'm nothing if not sensible."

They both said nothing for a few minutes, and Beth had the odd sense that Liz was checking her out? If it'd been anyone else, Beth would be confident.

"It was hard but once people were vaccinated, we opened our doors and we've done really well. Londoners love to go out and those who could came with great energy. It's been fantastic." Beth sighed, a long lingering outpouring of breath that embodied the weariness she felt.

"Fantastic? You sound tired."

"The new restaurant has added a lot more workload than any of us had anticipated. In the before times, we used to have quiet nights each week. Not anymore. Every night, the place is packed and while that is great for my pockets, it's hard on my back and legs to stand and walk all night."

"Can you take a night off?"

"Technically yes."

"So do that."

"I can't. Seraph's is my club." Beth breathed in and out slowly. "It's more than that. I've spent a long time without the energy of other people. If working makes me a little tired physically, it's worth it to be surrounded by people who are having a great time. On balance, I'd rather be in the club than away from it."

Liz nodded slowly. "Then rest now. Come on." She held out her hand and Beth took it. Liz's long fingers curled around Beth's palm and her touch was soft enough that she could feel the ridges of Liz's fingerprints against the thin skin near her thumb. Liz tugged a little and walked towards Beth's bedroom. If she didn't know Liz was demisexual and therefore potentially not physically interested in Beth, she would've assumed they were going to lie on the covers and kiss.

"Lie down."

Beth couldn't help it. She raised her eyebrows and winked. "So bossy."

"I'm not naïve, Beth. I know what you mean."

"And?"

"I'd like to kiss you again, but first you need to lie down and rest."

"Well…" Beth stumbled over what to say next. Her instinct was to blurt out something sarcastic to ease the growing anticipation in her chest. Her pulse raced at the notion of kissing Liz because her own attraction to Liz wasn't under any question. She'd beg for a kiss if she thought it would make any difference. She wanted to take a kiss from Liz, but instead she'd let her lead.

There was one way she could make her own needs known, and she flung herself on her bed and spread her arms out wide above her head. Her shirt slipped upwards, and she wriggled her hips a fraction to draw attention to her cute boy-cut panties. They were mostly lace and she loved the way they spread over her arse.

"Stop that. You need to rest first."

"Again with the bossiness." Beth saluted Liz and winked again. Anything to distract her from the way her skin tingled in hope and her heart raced.

"What about your leg?"

"What about it?"

"On or off?"

"Leave it. I don't intend to rest for long."

Liz sent her a scathing look. "Don't you?"

"Make me." Teasing like this came naturally to Beth and from the way, Liz's eyes widened slightly, and her cheeks pinked, she wasn't completely averse to it. Interesting. It was time to take a risk. "Kiss me."

Liz tilted her head to the side and slowly raked her gaze over Beth's reclined body. Liz's long glances sent shivers of hope flitting over Beth's skin. Her pulse quickened and her breath shortened.

"I think I might," Liz said.

Beth sat up. "Please?"

"You fascinate me, Beth. Queen B." Liz walked around the bed, closer to where Beth sat, then sat beside her. The bed dipped a little under her weight and Beth shuffled closer until they were only inches apart and the warmth of Liz's breath touched her lips.

Beth waited, not wanting to push into Liz's space. She always preferred her partners to direct her, and she especially loved the agony of this moment. The waiting, the uncertainty of not knowing if the other person wanted this, and the way tension built until someone moved first. Most especially, she loved it when the other person made the first move.

"Can I kiss you?" Liz asked.

"Yes please." Beth didn't move. Her breath rasped slightly on each iteration, and her heart thumped with anticipation in her chest, beating against her breast bone like the hammers on piano strings.

It was several delicious breaths before Liz lifted her hand and cupped Beth's cheek. The touch—so simple—made Beth damp and she shuffled slightly on the bed readjusting the way she sat. The last thing she wanted now was pins and needles, or for her leg to be more uncomfortable than usual.

The intensity of Liz's gaze, with her blue eyes observing her, tore Beth's attention away from ordinary concerns. That gaze screamed need and sex and Beth wanted it all.

Beth licked her bottom lip; it was dry from so many concurrent breaths rushing over it. When Liz used her thumb to trace over her lip, following the pathway of Beth's tongue, a shockwave of heat spilled through Beth's body, hotter than she had felt in a long time. She barely had time to dwell on why such a straightforward touch thrilled her, when Liz—finally—leaned closer and kissed her. Her lips were as soft as the first time, but this time, it was better because Liz led the dance between them.

Beth felt her eyes roll back in her skull at the sheer pleasure of being thoroughly kissed and she fought to keep them open. She didn't want to miss a moment of this; of the way Liz kissed with impunity and desire and hunger for her. This kiss had been worth waiting for. All the tension between them, all the moments of friendship… it all combined into a searing connection which tasted like cinnamon, oats, and brown sugar—sweet and succulent and richly warm—and the incredible luxury of Liz. Something like elderberry flowers or a very floral gin. Decadent. Beth couldn't believe her incredible good fortune that this kiss was happening to her. She'd had many kisses since Jewel had died, but all of them faded away, pale and insipid compared to this moment. Beth often lived in the moment, yet this one was different. More colourful and full of flavour and intensity, as if it were special. She jerked away.

"Did I do something wrong?"

"No." Beth struggled to find her voice. Even with her face several inches away from Liz, her body still beat in the needy rhythm like tap shoes clicking out rapid beats on the floor.

"Can I kiss you again?"

Beth nodded, unwilling to trust her voice. What she wanted to say was, 'only if you want to be ravished' because as much as Beth adored being led by her partner in bed, she couldn't wait any more. She desperately needed to touch Liz. Everywhere. She needed to taste her slick juices and pump her fingers inside until she clenched around her. She wanted Liz to cry out.

All thoughts fled, replaced by reality, as Liz kissed her again. This time with renewed urgency, as if she'd only been exploring cautiously before. Now Liz kissed her with confidence and knowledge, and Beth revelled in it. The wait was over and reality was better than she'd thought possible. She wrapped her hands around Liz's head, threading her fingers through her long hair. It was all tightly pulled up into a bun, and Beth loosened it as she clutched tight to Liz. The contrast between them was as hot as Hades, with Beth still in her sleeping shirt and panties, with unkempt bed hair, and Liz neatly dressed in the elegant blouse and shirt she wore last night with her hair wound tightly in a bun.

Slowly they fell together until they lay back on the bed, cuddled up together, both on their sides, with lips still locked in a never ending kiss. Or at least, Beth didn't want it to end. She wanted to be kissed like this every day. She slid one hand down Liz's spine, tugging her slightly, because she wanted Liz to roll on top of her.

"What are you doing?"

"I want your weight on me." Beth wanted to be pressed into her bed, preferably with Liz's thigh between her legs.

"Like this?" Liz moved quickly and Beth sighed as Liz covered her body, exactly how she liked it.

"Oh yes."

Liz giggled and Beth felt it right inside her chest. Liz wore too many clothes although they did nothing to hide the way their boobs were squashed together. Every rumble of Liz's laugh had a direct line to Beth's aching nipples.

"What is funny?"

"Nothing."

"But you laughed."

Liz kissed her, a brief brush of lips. "You are a joy. The few people who try to understand my demisexuality and then stick around for me tend to assume that I'll be passive in bed. It's not like that. I need emotional connection before I feel physical connection, but that doesn't dictate the type of connection I want. Not at all."

"And that's funny?"

"It's joyful that you didn't assume. You just told me what you wanted and let me decide what I want."

In that moment, Beth knew she was in trouble, because she was more interested in listening to what Liz wanted in bed than in fucking her. She still wanted to fuck her—a lot —that wasn't in question, but she also needed to know everything about her.

She wanted to know all the ways Liz wanted to fuck her and she wanted to do them. Today. Tomorrow. Every day. Beth sucked in a short breath between her teeth, and it whistled a little. This feeling had to be because it'd been weeks since she'd had sex with someone else and she was greedy for it. That was it, nothing more. She didn't need to add unnecessary emotions to this moment.

"Then kiss me, touch me. I'm yours to direct." Sex was something Beth knew. She could enjoy being here now with Liz without worrying about anything else. Being in the moment was Beth's strong point, it was her way of enjoying the good times. If this pandemic had taught her anything it was that Mama and Jewel were both right. Good and bad follow each other in cycles, therefore the good needs to be enjoyed while it exists so the memories could hold her through the bad.

"I'm a little rusty. Please tell me if you are uncomfortable." Liz waited for Beth to nod, then she pounced. If the last kiss was strong, this one was wonderfully dominant. Beth was ragged for breath as Liz took charge of her mouth, her tongue thrust inside, stroking with impunity and she left no room for Beth to join the dance.

She was completely taken over and it was ... the fucking best kiss of her life. Almost too much, almost overwhelming in its ferocity, and yet not quite enough either. She followed wherever Liz led, because Liz was a competent dancer who knew all the steps and Beth could relax into her hold. Liz pressed her leg between Beth's and shoved her thigh hard against Beth's pussy. Beth gasped at the rough contact but Liz gave her no time to recover as she swiped her tongue through Beth's mouth again. Just as Beth wanted more, Liz dragged her lips down, over Beth's chin, down her throat, with kisses that nipped at her skin. Beth was alight, her skin on fire, and her hips bucked against Liz's thigh, needing more friction. More of her.

"Quiet." The command made Beth want to protest. Had she been loud? Liz pressed a finger over her lips and Beth tried to suck the digit into her mouth. She might like being led, but she wasn't going to be completely passive. Liz shifted, just enough that she could tug Beth's shirt over her head. Beth grabbed at Liz's shirt, needing skin against skin, but Liz batted her hands away.

"Patience."

"And if I say no?" Beth croaked between moans.

"Try it. I'll stop if you want."

"I don't want you to stop."

Liz cupped Beth's bare tits, pulling them together. She nuzzled into them, and Beth bent her neck so she could press a kiss to the top of Liz's head. Sensation flooded her as Liz sucked on her nipple hard, and Beth flung her head backwards onto the bed as she cried out. She had to do something with her hands, needed to touch Liz. She spread them greedily over Liz's spine, tugging desperately at her blouse until she touched her skin, as Liz sucked and nibbled and licked until Beth was writhing with need. Having Liz's mouth on her skin was amazing; worth waiting for.

15

Liz loved this moment, when her brain stopped arguing with her and she could sink into pleasure. She wanted to make this special for Beth; sex for her was always very specific and individual. She kissed a trail down Beth's taut stomach, admiring her fit form with muscles rippling under a soft layer of flesh. Once a dancer, always a dancer.

From Beth's lean body, it was easy to see how teaching other people to dance kept her fit and strong. Her skin tasted like warmth with little hints of the honeysuckle and vanilla from the laundry powder she must use for her sheets. Vanilla was one of Liz's favourite flavours and she breathed in against Beth's skin as she kissed her all the way to her cute lacy panties. She moved her weight again, allowing her to pull Beth's underwear down her legs.

"Spread yourself for me."

Beth wriggled in a way that had to be practised, removing one leg from her underwear, so they hung around her prosthetic. Then she obeyed Liz's command. It was glorious. Beth's exposed floral pink pussy was wet and lush and ready for her. Liz slid two fingers inside her, loving the way Beth moaned decadently. Soon she had Beth panting, and begging for more, and just as Beth looked like she would growl at Liz for taking so long, Liz bent her head and sucked Beth's clit.

Yes, she was perfectly delicious. So hot and sweet and succulent. Responsive too, and Liz licked and sucked until Beth shook with pleasure. Her curls were trimmed short, providing a roughness against Liz's mouth and combined with the slickness of her pussy to create the perfect textures.

"Please." The ragged way Beth begged was enough for Liz to be close to coming, and with one long lick, she shifted up along Beth's body. Liz kept her fingers inside Beth, leaving her hands squashed between their bodies, as she ground her own pussy against Beth's thigh and kissed her.

Beth moved quickly, their limbs and hands tangling as they tried to touch each other everywhere. Soon enough Liz flew over the edge, and Beth came with her.

"You are amazing," Beth sounded like she was winded, unable to breathe properly in the aftermath.

"Worth the wait?" Liz hated the sudden uncertainty when she should be enjoying the way Beth could barely breathe from the intensity of the orgasm she'd just given her. The uncertainty came, not from her physical abilities, but from not knowing Beth's emotional state. From now on, she'd be loyal to Beth, but in her experience, other people didn't combine the physical and the emotional in quite the same way that she did.

"Abso-fucking-lutely." Beth grinned and kissed her again. "Another round?"

Liz laughed, a relaxed loose laugh as all her qualms

disappeared at Beth's keenness. "I've heard that dancers have extraordinary stamina. Shall we test the theory?"

"Yes please." Beth's gaze was still soft and satisfied and Liz couldn't wait to see if she could make her eyes darken with pleasure again. She rolled onto her back and undid the buttons on her blouse.

"Let me help."

"No. I want you to watch." Liz was going to put on a show for Beth and it was going to be incredible, although judging by the state of her pussy, it wasn't going to take long either. The bed dipped under her as Beth shifted. Liz glanced up at Beth's face, her brown eyes following Liz's fingers. The last button proved a little difficult thanks to the way her fingers trembled slightly under the intensity of Beth's gaze. Finally it came free and she opened up her blouse to expose her bra. Liz thanked herself for choosing one of her favourite's last night, lilac lace that supported her full breasts.

"Can I touch you?" Beth asked.

"Yes." Liz wasn't sure what to expect and what she got from Beth was a slow exploration, tentative as she kissed Liz's bare skin along the edge of her bra. Her skin was hot with gooseflesh chasing Beth's kisses, and when Beth turned up the intensity with a scrape of her teeth, Liz cried out. She fumbled with her skirt, unzipping it, and lifting her hips to slide it down over her hips.

"You are gorgeous."

Liz believed Beth even though she didn't think so herself. "I'm fit enough from rambling, I suppose."

"Being beautiful has nothing to do with fitness or the way someone looks on the outside and everything to do with that you hold yourself. You are gorgeous because you know your own worth."

Beth climbed onto Liz's body, straddling her waist with her naked form. Remnant moisture from Beth's pussy was slick against Liz's stomach, creating a memory that teased, just as Beth teased by playing with Liz's breasts until she ached from the way Beth worshipped her. She groaned, wanting more, and Beth leaned down to kiss her. The kiss quickly became urgent, unbridled, and Liz couldn't breathe and didn't care. She'd happily suffocate in this kiss. Just as her lungs screamed for air and she was ready to pull away, Beth dragged her lips down over Liz's cheeks, gently skimming the skin until she sucked hard against Liz's galloping pulse at the base of her neck.

"You'll leave a mark."

"Do you want me to?"

"Maybe?" Liz found it a bit hard to concentrate on whether she wanted to be marked by Beth or not. It wasn't often that her brain stopped whirring, yet Beth's ministrations had managed the feat.

"Not today, then." Beth seemed to know just how much to push Liz without making her uncomfortable, and when she nipped Liz's ear lobe, Liz cried out. She reached out for Beth's hands, wanting to push them down between her legs, and Beth let her. Beth slid lower, her thighs resting just above Liz's knees, and she let Liz move her hands to where she needed them. Liz pressed Beth's thumb against her clit, hard. It was—frustratingly—not quite enough.

"What would you like, Liz?" The question came with another bite to her earlobe and Liz mewled as Beth's teeth scraped over her sensitive skin.

"I want to come."

"Now?" Beth kissed her on the lips, then waited, hovering just above Liz's face.

"Yes." She breathed in deep and sent Beth her most commanding stare. "Now."

Beth pulled her hands away from Liz's and Liz frowned. She wanted to come, not to have Beth remove her hands from her pussy. She growled and Beth grinned, raising one eyebrow. Liz opened her mouth to remind Beth of what she wanted, but nearly bit her tongue when Beth raked her blunt nails over Liz's stomach, then plucked her nipples hard. Heat and pleasure flooded her body and Liz cried out, loud enough to wake the neighbours if they were home. Her cheeks flushed with embarrassed heat in a strange contrast to the rest of the heat making her veins steamy with pleasure. She barely had time to figure this all out when Beth slid her hands under Liz's lilac lace lingerie and inside her soaking wet heat.

"You feel amazing. So slick and hot." Beth pumped her fingers, using her thumb to massage Liz's clit. It was the last rational thought Liz had before a flush spread over her body, and she clenched everywhere. Pleasure spiralled through her, and she came hard, hips bucking, and Beth rode her thrashing body with a sly satisfied grin on her face. Liz reached for her and pulled her down against her for a hug. Beth's hands were caught between them and the hug was awkward but it didn't matter. Liz wanted to be as close to Beth as physically possible.

· · ·

The ringtone on her phone woke her and she found herself tucked under a blanket on Beth's bed. She sat up and glanced around the room for her phone, finally finding it on the bedside table. By the time she'd grabbed it, she'd missed the call, so she put it down again and got out of bed to find Beth.

"How long did I sleep?"

"Twenty minutes or so." Beth was watering her plants. She'd gotten dressed and was wearing jeans paired with a bright red halter neck top.

"Why are you dressed like you are going out?"

"I have to go do work soon."

"Oh, of course." Liz probably should go home. "I'll leave you to it, then." She went back to Beth's bedroom and gathered up her clothes and put them on again. Doing that reminded her of the way she'd taken them off and a hot shiver tore down her spine. If Beth didn't have to work, Liz would happily keep her in bed for the next week. It wasn't until she had kissed Beth goodbye and she was in a ride share car on her way home that she listened to the voice mail the earlier caller had left. All the sated pleasure in her limbs fled as her lawyers outlined the problems with the settlement on the neighbouring building. No. She needed to get this sale sorted. She didn't want her deposit returned. She wanted to own the building so she could give her darling Beth everything she wanted. Nothing else would get in the way of this problem until it was solved.

16

———

Beth didn't hear from Liz for over a week. At first the breathing room had been good. Sex with her was incredible but also a little intense and she didn't want to rush things. They were friends. Technically they were more than that, friends with benefits, and Beth didn't want this flame to burn brightly then disappear.

In her experience when sex was intense, any time spent together would ultimately be short lived. Short sharp affairs with people who were essentially strangers was one thing. To have the same with a friend had the potential for hurt when it inevitably ended—because these things always came to an end—then their friendship would become awkward and stilted. Sex with Jewel hadn't been like this... Or had it? It was so long ago, she could barely remember what it had actually been like. Her memories had given her a steady picture of her relationship with Jewel, but were they real? Or had time melted them all together and given her a memory of Jewel that was rose coloured and gentler than reality?

A ding from her phone was a welcome relief from her thoughts.

Liz: How are you?

Beth: Busy. You?

Liz: Sorry I've been missing in action. Some stuff with work came up.

Beth shrugged. It wasn't really her business what Liz did when they weren't together. They'd slept together once. It hardly constituted a relationship.

Beth: No worries.

Liz: Can I call?

Beth replied with a thumbs up emoji, and her phone rang.

"Thanks so much. Are you well?" Liz asked.

"Why are you thanking me for a simple call?"

"I basically disappeared for a week and I thought you might be mad at me for doing that."

"No. I'm good."

It was just sex, hardly worth all the overthinking on Liz's part.

Liz breathed out heavily in her ear. "I'm so glad. I had a big problem at work and it just absorbed me. Before I knew it, a whole week had gone by and I hadn't talked to you."

"It's fine really." It wasn't like they were in a relationship and Liz had a habit of disappearing without notice. "Were you safe?"

"Yes." Liz gasped. "Were you worried about me? I should've sent you a text."

"Liz. I'm your friend. You don't owe me a text if you are busy."

"Oh? But we…"

"Had sex? It still doesn't mean I want to check up on your whereabouts."

"That's confusing."

"It's really not. If we lived together and you disappeared for a week without warning, I'd be stressed, but that's not the case here. You are independent and perfectly free to do whatever you want without informing me."

"Okay?"

"Did you call for a reason?" Beth probably shouldn't push Liz's buttons like this but it was too tempting since Liz didn't seem to know what she wanted from Beth. It seemed clear enough to Beth; they were online friends, Liz was her landlady, and they had fucked once. It didn't need to be more complicated than that. A giggle caught in her throat. It was already pretty bloody complex. What was she doing fucking her landlady who was also her friend? Disaster lay down that road, and if she was advising a friend in this situation, she'd tell them to walk away now before it went sour.

"No reason. I just wanted to hear your voice."

The satisfying warmth that filled her chest at being wanted was why Beth wouldn't take her own advice. "I'm here whenever you want to talk."

"Can I ask you a favour?"

Seriously? So much for being wanted for herself. Hopefully Liz wasn't going to be one of those fair weather friends who only called when they needed something. Not that Beth had any reason to believe that might be true, but she'd met a lot of people in her life and there was always a chance, especially given the way they'd met.

She was being unfair. Liz had gone out of her way to help Beth keep Seraph's. Still…

"Are you asking as my friend, my landlady, or…" Beth let her voice trail off on purpose.

"Friend."

"Ask away." Doubts aside, Beth liked helping her friends.

"Um, it's awkward."

"Liz. I've seen you naked. Nothing is awkward after that." It wasn't true; plenty of things could be awkward after sex, but Beth hoped that the throwaway saying would help ease Liz's obvious worry about whatever it was.

"Would you like to come to my fiftieth birthday party?"

Beth grinned, pinching her lips together so she didn't burst into laughter. She'd really twisted herself up with all that overthinking, and it was just a bloody party. There was nothing awkward about a birthday party, unless Liz was nervous about the big five-oh.

"Absolutely. You are my friend, of course I'd want to celebrate with you. It sounds great. When?"

"Excellent. I'm glad you want to come and well, this is a bit odd, but I don't know when or where. My friends Gita and Matias are organising it. Can I give your details to them?"

"Sure. No problem. Steph can run Seraph's for whatever night it's on, assuming it's going to be a night time thing."

"I don't know. Like I said, they haven't given me any details. Gita only wanted a list of people I wanted to invite."

"Is it a surprise party?"

Liz laughed. "Well, hardly, if they've asked me about it. I suppose the location and date could be? I don't much like surprises, so I'd be a bit annoyed if friends who've known me for years gave me a surprise party. It sounds like a nightmare."

"I'm sure your friends understand. Can I ask a question?"

"Yes."

"Why do you feel awkward about inviting me to your party?" Beth hoped it wasn't because they hadn't defined their relationship.

Liz made an odd sound. "If I don't know what is planned, then I don't know what you'll be walking into. What if it's weird for you?" It sounded like Liz was worried about how Beth would cope in a room full of strangers. If that was it, it really was no concern at all. Beth worked in hospitality, surrounded by strangers all the time, and she loved it.

"It'll be fine. I love a good surprise myself, as long as it comes from a kind hearted place. If you aren't too busy, drop by the club for a drink tonight and we can chat about it."

"Okay. That sounds lovely."

Beth took a chance. "And bring an overnight bag. It's Monday tomorrow and we don't open, so I can stay in bed all day if I want."

The rough way Liz cleared her throat echoed through the phone, telling Beth she was going to get laid tonight. Sweet! She'd forgotten that part of being in a relationship. Good sex on tap whenever she wanted without having to filter through a group of people and then taking a chance on whether someone had any skills.

"I don't want a late night." Or maybe not.

"It's completely your choice, but I can give you the key to my place if you want and you can go to bed whenever you want." Beth didn't usually invite people to sleep over, preferring to invite them upstairs for sex, then send them on their way. However, the sex with Liz had been the best she'd had in a long time and she wanted a repeat. Seriously though, Liz had already slept in her bed a couple of times before they'd fucked. Whatever. To ascribe anything emotional to this invitation was silly, except a cold chill touched the back of Beth's neck. This was going to hurt more than usual when it ended. She rubbed away the chill. She'd deal with that when it happened. For now, she was going to enjoy herself. Life had taught her to grab happiness because bad things happened whether you took risks or were cautious. It was too late to worry about falling in love with Liz and what might happen if they decided this wasn't going to work out. The potential for being hurt was no reason to avoid fun. She wasn't going to miss out on being with Liz and her fantastic mouth. She'd survived worse than a little friendship break up.

"Thanks. I like that plan. See you later."

"Later."

Only a few minutes after the call ended, Beth's phone dinged with a new message.

Unknown: Hi, I'm Gita. Liz's friend. She said I could talk to you about organising her 50th?

Beth: Sure. I have a few minutes now if you want to call.

Sure enough, her phone rang.

"Hi Beth. Gita here."

"Hi."

"Liz mentioned that you own a club. I know this is a bit forward, but I was wondering if we could book it out for the whole evening for Liz's birthday."

Beth did a quick calculation. Before the pandemic, they'd done this on occasion, usually on an evening that was typically quiet. "We aren't open on Mondays, so that would be simple to organise and at a base rate that covered our staff and other expenses. Any other day would be more expensive as I'd need to ensure we don't lose out from being open."

"Could you send me some options?"

"Absolutely. Can you text me your email address? And perhaps a budget?"

"Sure. Consider it done. Thanks for that."

"Anytime."

"Cool, cool. I'll send you a text." Gita hung up and Beth let out the breath she didn't know she'd been holding. Liz's friends wanted to hire the whole club for her fiftieth? How many of them were there? If Liz knew, then it made sense that she asked if it might be awkward, but why not just say so? That left with Beth with two options; either Liz knew and she felt weird about it in which case Beth should say no to holding the party in the club, or Liz didn't know and she was worried for another reason.

This was why Beth wasn't keen to rush back into a relationship with anyone. Misunderstandings tended to blow up in emotional dramas and she was too old and set in her ways to have that in her life again. She had too much to do at Seraph's to worry about any of that nonsense. Once Gita's email arrived, then she could work out a budget, and maybe there was an opportunity in the idea. She parked it to the side until she had more information. In the meantime, there was a different consideration to discuss with her team.

"Hey Steph."

Her bartender stopped cutting up citrus and leaned on the bar. "Yeah?"

"I'm thinking about changing the scheduling. I'd like to close on Tuesdays as well."

"It's a pretty quiet night, and it'd be nice to have more time off, although they still make a profit, don't they?"

"Yes. It's not a big one, but yes, Tuesdays still make more than they cost."

"You're the boss. What brought this on?"

"I've had someone offer to rent the whole club for a birthday party, and I wonder if that would be a better use for Tuesdays."

Steph drummed her fingers on the bar. "You know what would be better?"

"What?"

"We could put a calendar on the website for private events and give people the options of every Tuesday and every second Thursday, as well as weekend lunches."

"Why every second Thursday?"

"Charlie has been complaining that it's too hard to find enough dancers for Thursday's open stage nights and I wonder if it would be better if we had less of them."

Beth tried not to frown. Why hadn't Charlie talked to her about that? "I'll talk to Charlie."

"Don't blame her for not saying anything. She's been trying to find a solution without bothering you because you've had a lot on your plate lately."

"Okay." Beth was more disappointed that Charlie obviously felt she couldn't talk about work problems with her, than she was with the actual problem. "I really like the weekend lunches idea. I'll run it past Jonti with regards to food because catering an event might be different to the pop up restaurant he's been doing, and we'd also have to work out timing so they don't run against each other." It would be easier once the restaurant had its own space. Once again, thinking about business plans forced her to think about Liz, not that it was a problem now she knew what she tasted like. Tonight beckoned.

"You're right about Tuesdays being quiet. It's not just that night. We've certainly seen a drop off in people coming out lately. I think everyone is starting to get back to their old routines and they don't have the same compulsion to get out of their houses as they had at first."

"I suspect you are right. I'll have a closer look at the numbers." Beth had been so busy with the everyday tasks that she hadn't had time to do analysis lately. "Do you need any help?"

"No, I'm fine. Reiko will be here soon. Go and crunch numbers, boss." Steph grinned and Beth nodded.

"Thanks." Working with spreadsheets wasn't her favourite thing. It'd been a necessary skill she'd had to learn when she'd started the club. Tracking the door numbers and bar sales had become a habit that helped her keep a handle on her business, but the restaurant had taken up so much time lately that it'd been several weeks since she updated her numbers.

Liz sat in her usual spot at the bar, musing on the idea that she already had a usual spot. It was at the end, near the display of potted plants. The heart philodendron was so lush and healthy. Why didn't hers look like that? She'd been here for nearly an hour, nursing her Gin and

Tonic, slowly scanning the room over and over for Beth without success.

"Just ring her," the bartender suggested.

"It's Steph, isn't it?"

"Yes."

"Won't she be busy?"

Steph chuckled. "She's always busy. My guess is that she's still stuck at her computer doing business crap or whatever. I'm sure she'll appreciate the break."

"If you are sure?"

"I'm sure. Beth invited you here. Let her know you have arrived."

Liz thanked Steph and dialled Beth's number. Is that what people called it now days with smart phones? She was old enough to remember having a rotary dial telephone, although her parents had been some of the first to get the new touch-tone button phone in the early 80s.

"Liz," Beth answered after only one ring.

"I'm down in the club, waiting for you."

"Okay. I'll be down in a bit."

Liz could hear the tapping of a keyboard in the background. "Are you busy?"

"I've just been doing paperwork. See you soon."

Liz replied in kind, then waved at Steph for another drink. Two gins in one night was a little excessive, although she easily justified it to herself because she didn't drink every night. Her parent's views on alcohol consumption continued to influence her and that was probably a good thing for her health. Tonight, she could make an exception as she needed it to settle the churn in her stomach. She blew out a long breath, imagining her mum scolding her for using alcohol to calm her nerves. The usual pang of grief came with the memory and she closed her eyes for a second, thankful to have her mum's pragmatism still keeping her safe and healthy. Besides, it was silly to be nervous. Beth was her … what? Girlfriend? They hadn't really discussed it. Liz felt far too old to have a girlfriend. It was such a juvenile word, really. Or perhaps she should embrace it as it brought a sense of youthful energy to them both. She shrugged. Musing on it was one way to fill the time.

"Liz." Beth's arrival jerked her out of her questioning, and she turned. Her breath caught in her throat. Beth looked incredible, a commanding presence even though she wore her usual style. Jeans with a loose shimmering top that drew Liz's attention to her stunning breasts. Sex with Beth had really turned her head and she wanted more. She'd already been partly in love with Beth before they'd slept together, and now she was a lost cause. Girlfriend? No. She wanted Beth to be her wife.

"It's so good to see you." Beth kissed her on the cheek and Liz's face warmed. "You blush so prettily."

"Hello." Liz couldn't find any words. They were all stuck on her tongue. "Beth."

"Shall I get you a drink?"

"Steph has already served me."

"Excellent." Beth grinned. "I'm pleased my staff are looking after you."

Liz's chest swelled. She must be special to Beth for her to have given her staff that instruction.

"Steph has been great."

"Brilliant. If you don't mind, I'll just pop into the

kitchen and see how Jonti is going, then we can take your things up to my place. Will you be okay here alone?"

"I can entertain myself." Liz winked, suddenly feeling brave thanks to Beth's declaration—of sorts—that she was someone special in her life. "I'll just ask Steph to tell me everything about you."

Beth grinned. "Sassy! I like it. Ask away. I have no secrets." Beth spun on her heel and walked away, quickly disappearing through a door beside the bar. Liz loved watching Beth walk, she had such an elegant efficient stride, a combination of being a dancer but with her own unique unevenness from her prosthetic.

Without knowing about it, Liz might have assumed that Beth had a long term knee injury or something that impacted on the smoothness of her stride. Being a rambler, she spent a lot of time watching people walk and it fascinated her to see how different people moved. Liz wanted to buy Beth some hiking boots and take her on all her favourite rambles. England and Scotland had so many places of natural beauty and Liz knew that Beth would rather Liz overestimate her ability and let her make her own decisions than to assume she could only manage the most accessible pathways. Accessibility was something the rambling club should put more effort into; there was no reason why everyone shouldn't enjoy the outdoors in their beautiful countryside. No reason, bar poorly maintained paths and maps that weren't specific enough with regards to steps or roughness.

"Did I hear my name?" Steph asked.

"You must have incredible hearing. You were down at the other end of the bar, serving people."

"It's an acquired skill. Years of working in a bar have given me plenty of practice at picking out people's voices over all the other noise."

"Have you always worked here?"

"No. Only for the last five years. It's the longest I've been anywhere. Beth is a great boss."

"She seems very hands on."

Steph's eyebrow raised up and Liz belatedly realised the euphemism. "Wait a sec." Steph rushed off to serve a couple of customers, chatting to the other two people working behind the bar as she went. She juggled several conversations and her hands flowed as she poured drinks, tapped on the screen, and sorted out payments.

"How's that drink?"

"I'm fine. This is more than enough for me for one night."

"Fair enough. I can get you some water if you want. Or tell you stories about Beth."

Liz leaned closer. "I'm not sure I want to know." It seemed wrong to snoop like that, but she was so, so curious. She wanted to know everything there was to know about Beth. "Who am I kidding? Please tell me something."

Steph grinned. "I knew you were curious." She glanced at the ceiling for a second. "This is a good one. On my first night here, Beth sent me out the back to clean the stock room. It was bloody funny because I found a smeared print of someone's arse-cheeks in the dust on top of the ice machine. I mean, I've worked in hospitality for my whole career, but that was a first for me."

"What do you mean? Had someone been…" Liz tried to

imagine why there would be a butt-shaped smear in the dust.

"Someone had been sitting on the ice machine. I went to tell Beth about it, and you know what she said?"

"What?"

"'That's why we need better staff. If it was clean, Anne's girlfriend wouldn't have had any dust to disturb.'" Steph cackled. "It was then that I knew this would be a fun place to work, because the boss didn't blink an eye at queer sex in the stock room."

"It sounds very unhygienic." Liz glanced down at her glass, unsure if she wanted to drink from it if the cleaning standards weren't very good.

"Well, that was the second thing Beth said. She dragged Anne into the stock room and made her clean the whole thing, and then we were all called to a meeting and told in no uncertain terms that if we were going to fuck people, it shouldn't be while we were on the clock, and it shouldn't be anywhere near the food or drinks. Our customers' good health is the most important thing. People come here to be entertained, not to get ill."

Liz let out a gentle breath of relief to hear that Beth cared for people like that. She could sip her drink without worrying about cleanliness. "And this Anne person?"

"She didn't stick around long after that."

"No, I imagine that was quite embarrassing."

Steph laughed. "My advice to her was to own it. Tell everyone, fuck yeah, it's my arse imprint, my girlfriend was eating me out in the stock room. But she chose to slink off in shame instead."

"I imagine that being called out by the boss for being unhygienic was a factor too."

"I guess so. Beth made sure we didn't gossip too much, but damn, if Anne was embarrassed by the whole thing, perhaps she shouldn't have had sex in the stock room. People always find out that kind of thing when we are all working together like this. Plus, I don't get why she was embarrassed. Beth was kind about it, and you know, her girlfriend must've been a good fuck if they were so desperate to do it on the ice machine. It's not the most comfortable place to get off." Steph chuckled, then slid a glass of water across the bar to Liz before hurrying off to serve someone else. Liz only sat alone for a moment before Beth turned up again.

"Come on, let's head upstairs now before it gets busy again. Steph will watch your drink for you." Beth waved at Steph who took Liz's gin and placed it in the fridge behind the bar with a coaster over the top. Liz picked up her bag and followed Beth, her head still spinning at the story. Two things struck her; people were a lot more casual about sex than she was, and Beth was a good boss who cared for her staff and her customers.

17

———

Beth spent the walk to her flat thinking about kissing Liz. Liz had left her long hair loose tonight and it framed her face really well. Her strong Scottish features with sharp cheekbones, slightly too big nose, and round eyes were softened by her hair. Usually she wore it pulled back sharply into a very business-like bun and Beth quite liked this version of her, slightly unbuttoned and casual. Tonight Liz wore plain black pants and a soft cashmere cardigan over a satin blouse.

Beth unlocked her flat and walked inside, aware of Liz's presence just behind her. Liz placed her bag in the same place as the last time she'd been here.

Should she get a proper place for Liz to put her things? No, that was getting well ahead of herself. This was likely just temporary, even if it felt more important than a hook up because she had invited Liz to stay the night instead of intending to send her home in a ride share car like she usually did with her hook ups. It was so natural to have Liz stay that she hadn't really thought about not doing it. It hadn't been intentional. It'd just evolved to this point, and Beth wasn't mad about it.

"Is this your mother?" Liz pointed to the framed photo on the wall of Beth's mum.

"Yes."

"You look like her."

"Thanks."

Beth had the same physique as her mum, although her brown eyes and black hair came from her father's side who was biracial white and Sri Lankan.

"She was a ballerina?"

"Yes. She danced for the Northern Ballet in Leeds as a soloist but was prevented from becoming a principal dancer due to knee issues."

"That must have been frustrating for her."

Beth nodded. "Yes. And back in the eighties, ACL operations weren't as good as they are now, so the recovery time after each operation took a long time. Papa supported her as she tried to get back to dancing, but eventually it became obvious that she wasn't going to recover enough to even be a soloist. A dancer's career is short even without injury."

"Did she teach you?"

"Yes. She put a lot of energy into my own dancing career." Being an only child and the daughter of a professional dancer had resulted in a lot of pressure to perform but Mama hadn't been as intense as some of the other dance mums. Probably because she understood what it meant to be a professional dancer, and she had been reasonably good at balancing her own ambitions against Beth's needs.

"Did you enjoy it?"

"Absolutely. I love dancing, especially in front of an

audience. Mama always encouraged me to take my own path and do something else too, not just dancing, probably because she knew how hard it was to get paid to dance. When I took up burlesque, she called it my little rebellion but she was happy for me too."

"Rebellion?"

"Yeah. I love burlesque because the choreography is much freer than in ballet which is quite prescriptive. Mama understood that as well as the need to perform for an audience."

"Is she still around?"

"Yes. She lives in Leeds with her new partner." Beth's parents had drifted apart—lack of communication had been the biggest problem after her mother had been forced to quit dancing—and now both had new partners. She chatted to them once a week. It was lovely and polite and they'd been very supportive after Jewel's death. Papa had helped out when she'd started Seraph's, teaching her how to do her accounts and other business stuff. Without him, the paperwork would've been near on impossible. Beth hadn't taken any money from her parents, who didn't really have anything to spare, and besides, she'd been stubborn enough that she wanted Seraph's to be hers and hers alone.

"She must be very proud of you."

"Why?"

"For running a dance club."

Beth cackled. "Well, it's certainly not ballet, and I still get the occasional backhanded comment about how she would've preferred grandchildren to a business." Mama knew she was bisexual with lesbian preferences, but old heteronormative habits died hard.

"She doesn't know you are a lesbian?"

Beth paused, a natural instinct because the sad truth was that not everyone in the queer community reacted well to this news. "Technically I'm bisexual, not a lesbian."

"And I'm a demisexual lesbian. We are all what we are. Why does that matter to your mother?"

"Mama always hoped that being bisexual meant that I'd end up married to a man and give her grandchildren." Beth didn't blame her mother for thinking like that. She had been brought up in a world where that's what women did; they had a short career, then they got married and had children. Mama had pushed beyond that narrative by continuing to dance professionally after Beth's birth, and her favourite quote had been from the dancer Barishnikov who'd said, 'I do not try to dance better than anyone else. I only try to dance better than myself.'

Liz tilted her head and frowned. "Um, I don't think that's quite how it works."

"Thank you." Gratitude for Liz's understanding caught in Beth's throat, coming out in a croaked cough. "I have zero interest in having children. Can you imagine trying to bring up kids in a club like this?"

"No, but I never wanted children either. I don't even have a pet because I like to travel. Well, back when we could anyway."

"You can again."

"To some places. A lot of the world is still unvaccinated. I don't think it's fair to travel, even if it's to vaccinated places, until the whole world is able to travel freely too."

"I like that philosophy."

"Thanks. I'll stick to rambling locally until then." Liz

shrugged. "I suppose that having children doesn't exactly stop people from travelling. It's just not for me."

Beth rubbed Liz on the shoulder. "You don't need a reason to want something or not want something. No one asks men why they don't have kids."

Liz rolled her eyes. "Isn't that so true? I'm glad we both agree with regards to children."

"Yip." Beth stopped herself from mentioning that they weren't in a relationship—it was just fucking—because it didn't need to be said and it was good that they agreed on something so big.

"Not that it matters for me anymore. I'm almost fifty."

Beth grinned, glad to change the subject. "Your big five-oh birthday. We can definitely hold it here. That's what your friend Gita wanted to know. I sent her an email with all the options and dates but she hasn't got back to me yet."

"I'll ring her. I don't want her spending lots of money on the party. I'll pay."

"You two sort that out and get back to me." Beth didn't want to get involved with another money discussion with Liz. She was the bloody landlady, she could … well, nothing. Whatever. Her being the landlady should have no impact on the price her and her friends paid to rent the club for a party.

"Shall we go back down to the club?" Beth asked.

"Do you need to?"

"Not immediately." Beth pushed aside her responsibilities for one simple reason. Liz was in her flat, with a look of anticipation on her face. It was the easiest thing in the world to kiss her, achieved with two steps forward, the placement of her hand on Liz's shoulder, then leaning in and grazing her lips against Liz's mouth. Liz responded with enthusiasm, wrapping her arms around Beth's waist and pulling her closer.

Beth slid her hand up and threaded it through Liz's hair and deepened the kiss. Chemistry sizzled and crackled in her veins as they kissed. Kissing Liz was so fresh and new and yet Beth was overwhelmed with a sense of homecoming. She wanted to walk upstairs every night after a long evening at Seraph's and be welcomed home by Liz's kiss. The thump of her heart should scare her, and it certainly shouldn't be so invigorating. It didn't make sense to want Liz here like that. Beth hadn't let anyone into her emotional space since Jewel —content to keep people at a distance—because she couldn't even fathom being remotely domestic with someone else.

Until now.

Somewhere along the line, Liz had slowly infiltrated Beth's life as a friend, a business partner, someone who looked after her when she was tired, and who made her body sing with her touch and her kisses. It was all a little much.

Beth should stop this kiss now, before it all went pear-shaped and she ended up getting hurt. Should, would, could. What was a little hurt in this game of life? Beth preferred to chase after what she wanted, regardless of the risks. She knew what heart break and grief felt like and it was worth the highs that came before... This kiss was worth it.

"Shall we go to bed?" Beth asked, leaping in completely. This thing with Liz was already complicated. She could manage it all because it was just sex with a friend. Friends with benefits—people did that all the time without it becoming serious.

"I'd like that."

Beth walked to her bedroom with her head held high. She loved sex, loved the way being with someone made her pulse race and her skin alive from their touch. She could manage their friendship and keep Liz firmly in that space emotionally while also getting what she wanted in this sphere.

"How much time do you have?"

Beth spun around to see Liz leaning in the doorway of her bedroom. Her soft cashmere cardigan was pulled tight across her boobs, and she had her hip cocked to the side.

"Plenty." Beth's voice crackled a little and she swallowed.

"Really?"

"Why? Do you want to go quickly?"

Liz's eyes sparkled and she grinned slowly. "I'm just working out the parameters."

"I do love it when you use your business speech on me."

Liz's eyebrows shot upwards. "Do you now?" She hadn't moved, yet Beth could feel her proximity in the way her skin tingled, and her clothes suddenly felt too small.

"There's nothing better than seeing someone commanding come undone." Beth's stomach tightened as she waited to see what Liz would do. She didn't have to wait long. Liz strode over and stood before her, their bodies touching.

"Sit on the bed."

Beth sat.

"Take off your top."

Beth took it off, never taking her gaze off Liz's, except

for the short time when she dragged her top up over her face and cast it aside. Liz held her stare, her eyes blazing with heat and unsaid sexual tension. She leaned closer, then just as Beth thought they'd kiss again, Liz pressed her cheek against Beth's cheek, and whispered in her ear.

"Do you think I could make you come without touching your clit?"

"Why would you want to?"

A nip on her earlobe made her gasp and Beth wanted to retract her question. Liz's hot breath against the skin of her neck sent gooseflesh scattering across her skin.

"I like the challenge of it."

"I don't think it's possible." Beth called Liz's bluff, even though she was already damp and she knew it wouldn't take much to push her at least close to an orgasm. Before she could take her next breath, Liz pushed her onto the bed and sat on her thighs, sinking her weight onto Beth. The shift in position meant Beth's hands drifted down Liz's spine and she used them to hold onto her waist. The cashmere was soft under her palms, nice, but certainly not as nice as bare skin.

"Oh, you don't?" Liz leaned forward and kissed Beth. Thoroughly.

Until her lungs burned for lack of oxygen in the very best way and she wriggled under Liz's weight. All that did was remind Beth that she wore nothing above her waist but her bra while Liz was still fully clothed, and the disparity sent fresh waves of heat through her veins. She loved it when someone took charge. And Liz certainly did that.

"Listen to your pulse." Liz sucked on her neck, right where someone might take a pulse reading, then just as it began to hurt, she relaxed her lips and kissed soothing kisses to the same spot.

Beth was helpless under the assault of sensation, everything tingled, from the tip of her toes through her core and down her arms to her fingertips. Even her amputated leg tingled; which was a wonderful change from phantom itches. The thought was fleeting, pushed away when Liz held her hand and placed Beth's fingers against her own pulse. Beth felt her heart racing in double time. It matched the beat in her chest… She groaned. Of course, it did. It was her own pulse. The overwhelming way that Liz nuzzled against her neck and covered her body had frozen all her thoughts, and Beth loved it. She wanted more. She arched her spine, unable to be passive anymore.

"Settle."

"No."

Liz winked, kissed her once more, then ground her public bone against Beth's own. Liz half-sat up, shifting her weight just enough, and Beth breathed in deep with a hiss and a moan.

Fuck, she was so loud under Liz's ministrations. She was given no time to think as Liz pushed her bra out of the way and sucked on one of her taut nipples. Liz's long hair fell across Beth's throat, silky and soft, and Beth removed one hand from Liz's waist to thread her fingers through Liz's hair. Liz plucked at Beth's nipple as she continued to suck on the other one, sending shards of heat spiralling through her. With each pinch, Beth bucked her hips, needing more, and each time, Liz kept her weight hard against her. Pinning her down in the most delightful way.

"Oh, fuck." Beth couldn't bring herself to admit it, but if

Liz kept this up, she'd soon come. She could imagine the satisfied smug grin on Liz's face and she wanted to see it. If she didn't get her hands on Liz's skin soon, the tension would be too much. She moved, suddenly aware that she'd left her fingers on her pulse where Liz had left them. Beth brushed Liz's hair back off her face, tucking it behind her ear, so she could better see her expression as she nuzzled on Beth's boobs, then Beth pushed her hands under Liz's top, tugging frantically at her blouse.

"Who tucks in shirts?" she growled.

"I like to look neat and tidy."

"Let me undo you."

"Okay." Liz's concession was so hot.

Beth's fingers struggled with the fabric as she pulled it free from Liz's belted slacks and finally, finally, she was able to lay her palms onto Liz's skin. She held her waist and used her as leverage to push her hips up against Liz again. Liz licked all the way up Beth's neck and throat, then kissed her again. A desperate passionate open-mouthed kiss that lacked finesse, and yet was perfect because it told Beth that she wasn't alone in needing more. Beth kissed Liz back, tasting the gin on her tongue. She must've had it with a slice of lemon too.

The combination of Liz's weight on her core, her tongue stroking her own, and her fingers on her boobs was wonderful. Tension grew, and when Liz sucked Beth's bottom lip into her mouth at the same time as she ground her mound against Beth's pubic bone, Beth let go. Her eyes rolled back in her head and she gasped as the waves of heat came and came. She wanted to return the favour but her whole body went slack. Beth was barely aware of the way Liz rolled off her and lay beside her. Liz took Beth's hand and used it to cup Liz's nude mound, and Beth's eyes flicked open to stare needily.

"Your slacks?" Beth whispered, still not able to open her heavy eyelids.

Liz didn't answer with words, only by guiding Beth's fingers onto her clit. She was slick and wet and Beth let Liz move her hand for her. Together they rubbed Liz's clit until she was moaning. With each moan, Beth slowly came back to earth from her own orgasm. She shifted so she could kiss Liz while simultaneously she used her other hand to explore down over Liz's stomach and thighs. The fabric of her slacks provided a textural contrast and answered the mystery. Liz had opened the fly but left them on.

Beth pushed them further down Liz's legs, out of the way, so she could sink her fingers inside Liz. Liz spread her legs and groaned into Beth's mouth. Beth pumped her fingers deep, using her tongue in the same rhythm as they kissed. Colour splashed across Liz's face, and then she closed her eyes and came, clenching on Beth's fingers. Perfection. Beth kissed Liz on her forehead, and slowly pulled her hands away so she could rest them on Liz's waist.

"How was that?" Liz asked. They'd lain together in silence with only their ragged breathing making any sound, although Beth's pulse was still audible in her ears after feeling Liz come around her fingers.

"I'm impressed," Beth said.

Liz had made an outrageous claim, and then achieved it, and it was glorious. Beth wanted more.

"Good. There aren't many people I like to impress, but you are one of them."

"Okay?" Beth heard a weight in those words that she wasn't sure about. "I'm just me, you don't need to try to impress me. Simply being here in my bed and giving me orgasms is plenty."

Liz paused for a few breaths. "I can do that. You do know that you are worth it."

"Of course." Beth shrugged. Self-confidence wasn't something she had an issue with, she'd always known that she was valid and good at what she did. Determined. Jewel used to say she was too stubborn for her own good, whatever that meant.

"Do you really need to go back to work?" Liz grinned and Beth was sorely tempted to stay in bed for another round.

"Yes. Surely you understand. It's my business."

Liz's smile grew into a chuckle. "Steph said you were very hands on."

"Does that mean you want my hands on you?"

"Oh, definitely."

Beth leaned closer for another kiss, then reluctantly sat up. "You can come with me. Steph will still have the rest of your drink saved for you."

"If it's okay with you, I'd rather stay here. I shouldn't drink two gins in one night anyway."

"Ahh come on. Live a little dangerously." Beth had never denied herself anything of pleasure. Life was too easily cut short for that nonsense. From the way Liz winced, it was plain that she didn't agree.

"It's fine if you don't want to. Stay here." Beth stood up and went to grab her shirt. "Treat the place like it's yours, eat, drink, have a shower, whatever."

"Are you sure?"

"Yes. I don't expect you to follow me around at work." In fact, that would be kind of weird, even in a club like Seraph's. Beth had the sudden urge to dash out of the room.

Was she really contemplating a relationship with someone who didn't work the same hours as her? When would they see each other? She ground her back teeth together so she didn't shake her head. This wasn't a relationship. It was just friends with benefits and they'd find time whenever it suited them both.

"Wake me up for a kiss when you finish work," Liz said.

"Is that a command or a promise?" Beth would rather flirt like this than spend any more time in her head pondering the ins and outs of what this thing between her and Liz was and where it might or might not be going.

"It is what you want it to be. Have a good evening at work."

Beth nodded. "Thanks." She didn't mind being dismissed from her own house right now because she needed something to make her get on with the job and not just stay here and fuck Liz again. She wanted to taste her on her tongue and to lick her from her ankles to her throat. Later. She threw on her shirt and paced out of her bedroom, slightly surprised to realise that she hadn't even removed her jeans. Her boots were at the front door, lined up next to Liz's black leather shoes, another reminder of potential domesticity. Beth blew out a long breath. It was time to put on her boots and get to work.

18

B eth spent most of the evening behind the bar, chatting to customers, in her element, and yet, she wasn't focused on the work. Knowing that Liz was asleep in her bed distracted her mightily, and she swayed between it being a good distraction and a terrible one. Throughout the night shift, she caught up with each of her key staff and talked to them about opening nights and got their feedback on future planning. Her staff often saw the business from perspectives that were valuable to her.

"Charlie. Another successful night."

"Dan, Jack, and Yolande were the stars as always. Did you see Dan's new trick?" Charlie put together the program of dancers every night, usually anchored by Yolande's historical style dances, Jack's neo-burlesque with dramatic costumes created by his husband Ace, and Dan's circus tricks.

"The firesticks?"

"Yes. He's so brilliant. Ben says that he made Dan practice in the park to prevent him from burning any of his grandma's plant collection."

"I hope you had adequate fire protection up there on stage."

Charlie nodded. "Of course. We had two extinguishers and a couple of buckets of sand. Don't be so boring, Beth."

"It's not boring to worry about safety."

"I didn't mean that. It's frustrating that you are getting involved with all the tiny details after it's already done. Just let me do my job without the little backhanders." Charlie sighed. "I'm sorry, but fuck, girl, you need to get laid or something."

"Charlie." Beth rolled her eyes. "I'm fine."

"Trust me. Random hook ups aren't a long term solution. Been there, done that, am much happier now." Lately everyone at Seraph's had fallen in love and they'd all started bugging her about when it would be her turn.

"Back off."

"Yes, boss. There's no need to get angsty about it." Charlie shrugged one shoulder and grinned. "We all just want the best for you. You're a great boss and a wonderful mother figure to everyone who needs it."

Beth scoffed. "Yeah, old mother Beth, that's exactly how I want to be seen."

Charlie laughed riotously. "I'd love to see you happy, that's all."

"I am happy. I have a successful club. I've saved it from being demolished. What more could I want?"

"Love." Charlie kept grinning as if love solved all problems.

"Fuck off." Beth allowed herself a cynical little chuckle.

"I don't need love to live a satisfying life." She'd already had her one true love, not that she believed that there was only one person for someone in life. It was more that she wasn't ready to move beyond her current friends with benefits situation with Liz. The very idea bugged her for some unknown reason.

"Look, I get it. I thought I was happy with my life before I met Elle. Even after I met her, when we still had a casual thing happening, but the whole pandemic and shit changed everything." Charlie waved her hands in the air. "My life is better now."

"Please don't tell me she completes you? Charlie, you are my second in command. You don't need another person to make you feel valid. You're already enough." Was Charlie going to shut up about this whole 'love makes people better' stuff? Beth really didn't want to spend any time thinking about why this interrogation irritated her so much.

"No. I wouldn't go that far. I wasn't incomplete without her. I'm just happier now."

"That's great. I'm pleased for you." And she was. It was lovely to see her crew in happy relationships where they supported each other. "I'd much rather discuss the scheduling issues that you've been worried about. We also need to have a meeting to talk about hosting the Burlesque of the Year contest. It hasn't been run for a couple of years and I'd like to make sure we are involved with this year's event because it's going to be massive."

"I'm on the committee for the awards. I'll make sure I mention this club at the next meeting. And hey, don't worry about the scheduling stuff. Your suggestions the other day were great. I'll reply to your email."

"Thanks." Beth would much rather talk about work than Charlie's previous topic. No wonder she had been avoiding Charlie lately, to the detriment of her business. Crap.

"What about this Liz character? Steph says she's been hanging around a lot lately. Who is she?"

Beth glared at Charlie—so much for focusing on the job —although her stare was unlikely to stop her very popular MC from charging along, like a truck with no brakes.

"She's no one. A friends with benefits situation. It's not important." And probably not love. A chill raced across the back of her neck. Huh. Was she lying to herself? "Say what you like, Charlie, but I don't need to fall in love. I'm good."

Charlie winked. "I think you protest far too much."

It took Beth several breaths before she could respond. "Think what you like. I'm the boss and my personal life isn't your business."

Charlie threw her head backwards and roared with laughter. "As you wish."

"What?"

"We've been through a lot of tough times together, Beth. Seraph's might belong to you, but it's my baby too. I've fought for this business and this life as much as you have. And all through that, you've never once lied to me." Charlie paused and the longer it stretched on, the fainter Beth felt. "Until now. I think this Liz is more important than you want to let on."

"Why are you pushing so hard? Can't you just leave it alone?"

Charlie held up her hands. "Sure. I can leave it alone. Of course, if it didn't matter, you wouldn't protest so much."

Beth shook her head and walked away. She needed a stiff

drink after that conversation because the other option was to run home to bed and Liz. And Charlie's frustrating nonsense was going to make her overthink the whole situation far too much. It was too early to declare love or anything like that. It was a timing issue. They'd been friends online for the entirety of the pandemic; which had felt like forever when it was happening.

The issue was simple. This wasn't love. It was friends with benefits; excellent benefits that warmed her all the way through and made her thighs tingle in anticipation. Just because Liz was wrapped up in her life and business and was currently asleep in her bed waiting for her didn't mean anything.

Didn't it?

She marched over to the bar and was about to pour herself a drink so she could relax and think this over without anyone else's fucking opinions when she stopped.

Why the fuck was she planning to drink alone when she had Liz in her bed? Regardless of what Charlie or anyone else thought, she could manage her own life including how she dealt with Liz. What was the most important thing? Sex and then sleep. She closed her eyes for a moment.

Soon everyone would finish up the evening's work and go home to their own fucking true loves or whatever, and she'd be able to lock up, go upstairs, and slid into a warm bed next to a warm body. It sounded like heaven for her old bones. Her stump hurt more than usual tonight. Probably because she'd spent all night pacing around the place instead of looking after herself. If she didn't go to bed soon, she would burn out and that would be bad for Seraph's. Happy with her logic, she started her closing up routine and sent everyone home.

It was nearly an hour later as she slowly climbed the stairs, finally able to head home to bed, she gasped. What were the odds that Liz had overheard her discussion with Charlie? She leaned on the wall outside her flat, running through the whole conversation.

"*She's no one. A friends with benefits situation. It's not important. Say what you like, Charlie, but I don't need to fall in love. I'm good.*"

Without context, Liz might think that Beth didn't care. It was one thing to believe what she'd said, and another entirely for Liz to hear them out of context. She didn't want to hurt Liz. She didn't even know how Liz felt about what they were doing. Likely it wasn't love for her either, just two independent women enjoying each other's bodies. She shook off the melancholic worry. Liz had been safely tucked into her bed when Charlie had teased her until she blurted that all out with irritation. Coincidences and misunderstandings like that only happened in books, not real life. She opened her front door and went through her normal routine.

By the time she got into bed, the initial burst of stress had worn off, her pulse had returned to normal, but she still reached out cautiously to see if Liz was there. Her fingers brushed satin and warm skin, and that was enough to quiet the nonsense in her head before she drifted off into a deep sleep.

~

Liz wished she'd worn her coat when she'd ducked out this morning to grab them both breakfast. It was bloody cold with the autumn wind whipping between buildings and along laneways. She pushed open the door to Beth's flat, lugging her two Tesco carry bags with her.

Years ago, Liz had taken several cooking courses to learn how to cook properly and she'd grown to love it. Cooking for one person without getting bored required skills and she'd taken the time to acquire them for herself. Perhaps she'd gone a little overboard at the local shop this morning, but her signature scrambled eggs would be better with a fresh sourdough loaf and a few condiments. She didn't want to take the chance that Beth might not have a crucial ingredient.

"Oh. I thought you'd left." Beth sat casually in one of her two chairs, and Liz realised it was the first time she'd seen her without her prosthetic. Obviously she'd taken it off in bed and once during sex, but Liz had been distracted and hadn't really seen it. She loved that Beth felt comfortable being herself with Liz around, although…

"I grabbed a few things for breakfast."

"Okay." There was something tense in the way Beth stared at her.

"Hold on. Did you think I'd left without saying goodbye?"

"Never mind." Beth shook her head.

"You did. Why?"

"It's nothing."

Liz put her carry bags on the bench and walked over to

Beth. "It doesn't look like nothing. Did I do something wrong?"

"No. I did."

"Excuse me?" Liz's breath caught in her throat.

"I said some things to Charlie last night that weren't great and I feel like shit about it."

"So apologise. Charlie works for you, yeah? She'll understand." Liz was more confused than before, unable to connect Beth being worried about Liz leaving this morning with whatever she'd said to Charlie.

"It's not Charlie I need to apologise to."

"Oh? This sounds very complex. Should I make you breakfast and then we can talk about it?" Liz had no idea what was going on in Beth's head, but she did know one thing. Everything was better with food, and she loved cooking for people she cared about.

"Sure. I won't say no to being looked after."

Liz smiled as she quickly walked over to Beth and kissed her on the forehead. "Excellent. Just relax and I'll have my signature scrambled eggs served up soon. Coffee?"

"Yes, please."

Liz began hunting through Beth's cupboards for the pan she needed. She made the coffee first, testing her own with a sip, then carrying a mug to Beth. Now, it was time to cook. First, she cracked six eggs into a bowl, added a dash of cream, some pre-sliced garlic and onions—an extravagant time saving choice at Tesco today—and finally a bit of grated blue cheese. A sprinkle of chilli flakes and some salt and pepper added flavour, then Liz gave it a quick mix. She sliced up the sourdough, then lightly fried it in butter in the frypan, before putting it on plates. It would stay warm enough while she made the eggs. She added more butter, a little splash of olive oil, and some truffle oil—for a truly luxurious experience—to the pan and turned the heat down low.

Liz poured in the egg mixture, then slowly scrambled it, working it with a spoon from the edges to the middle of the pan, until it was cooked through and smooth. Turning off the heat to let it sit, she then sliced up some chives, before adding the eggs to the bread, and decorating with the chives.

"Here you go." Liz handed Beth her, quite frankly, social media worthy plate.

"It's amazing."

"Thank you."

"I didn't know you could cook."

Liz laughed. "Obviously I haven't starved in the thirty years I've lived alone." Aside from those couple of years with Petunia, she'd always lived alone, and now she was older, she had less patience for the annoying habits of other people. Even though she was certain that she loved Beth, she wasn't keen to live with someone else again. It'd have to be true love to compromise enough to let someone into her space. She tried not to gasp as she realised one of the things she loved about Beth was how easily she had welcomed her into her home.

"Sure, but there's cooking to survive and then there's this sort of cooking. What else don't I know about you?"

"There are lots of things we don't know about each other." Liz jumped on the excuse to focus on the moment and not the future.

"Yeah." Beth didn't sound pleased about that, and Liz frowned.

"We have plenty of time to find out. It doesn't matter, you know."

"I guess so. What are we doing here anyway? It's friends with benefits, yeah?" Beth hadn't touched her food yet.

"Are the eggs not suitable?" Liz changed the subject. If Beth thought they were only friends with benefits, then obviously Liz was more deeply invested than Beth, and that was … disappointing. This always happened. Once she liked someone enough to have sex with them, it was a short ride to falling in love. Even when things had ended with previous partners, she still remained friends with them, although the friendships tended to fade with time as the other person drifted away from her.

"Huh?"

"You haven't touched your food."

"Oh." Beth picked up her knife and fork and began to eat. "It's delicious. Wow."

Liz wanted to satisfy Beth like this every day—so much for not wanting her in her space—but experience taught her to wait. She didn't want to scare Beth away with her intensity of feelings while this was so new and fresh. Ultimately it didn't matter how it all turned out between them. Now that Liz was this invested in Beth's wellbeing, she'd stay loyal for as long as Beth wanted. Loyalty was her super power.

"I'm serious. This is incredible." Beth shook her head as if she was going to say something more, but then kept eating and Liz waited. She may as well finish her food too. The truffle oil really did add that little something special to make it taste like luxury in her mouth, and she'd gotten the heat balance right with a good amount of chilli.

"Who is your favourite burlesque dancer?" Liz wanted to

know everything about Beth, and this seemed like an easy way to start a conversation.

"Now, or historically?"

"Whichever."

"Josephine Baker! She danced in the 1930s. She was the first Black superstar dancer in Europe. Totally awesome and made a shit-ton of money."

"Wow."

"Yeah. She challenged a lot of the early notions about burlesque and how dancers should look a certain way. I guess, in my own small way, I want to continue that progress at Seraph's by encouraging dancers with a range of body types."

"That sounds good."

"I hope so." Beth frowned.

"What's the matter?"

"Before my accident, I thought improving diversity was merely about being more inclusive with regards to race and gender. After my accident, I started to notice that all dancers were a similar height and shape. Not too tall, not too short, and certainly always slender. Long limbs, and most obvious of all, everyone was able-bodied. There were no amputees dancing. I'm not proud that it took something so drastic for me to notice."

"Life is a journey." Liz wanted to say something more useful than a simple platitude but she didn't know what might be more useful.

"Whatever. The important thing is that we all have unconscious biases and privileges that we need to learn to acknowledge. I'm embarrassed that it took an accident for me to see some of mine."

Liz opened her mouth to support Beth, but she waved her hands and Liz swallowed the comforting words down again.

"Yes, I get it. I'm trying to fix things now that I see the problems, but it's not enough. It'll never be enough."

"It will." Liz paused. "You must have learned a lot of those biases from your mother, since she was a dancer too."

"Mama always struggled with maintaining the weight required to be a soloist with her company, and many of her eating habits were—" Beth breathed in slowly. She really didn't want to go into the detailed way Mama counted calories.

"Passed on to you?" Liz guessed.

"Yes. I was lucky in many ways, as Papa always ensured Mama stayed healthy and when she put too much control around the amount of food she was eating, he was able to help her relax. She was more of a chronic exerciser to control her body and weight, rather than someone who had an actual eating disorder, although many doctors would argue there isn't much of a difference. It's all about rigid control over her body. She still struggles now, even though she's nearly seventy."

"These things are always complex."

"What do you know about it?"

"My parents were both doctors. They often worked in areas of the world with poverty and famine, and we talked a lot about nutrition."

"That's very different to possible eating disorders."

"Yes, although it's a myth that eating disorders are a first world problem. Poverty creates a lot of physical and mental health issues and they manifest in all sorts of complicated ways."

Beth smirked. "If I ever doubted it when you said your parents were doctors, you've just proven it completely. I bet you went to a posh school."

"Yes." She had gone to an expensive boarding school. "What do you mean?"

"You speak like you are reading a fucking textbook. Manifest. Sure. Look, all I know is that Mama was under a lot of pressure to maintain her weight and physical health in certain ways and the result was that she was very precise about what she ate and how that impacted on the amount of exercise she needed to do in response to her intake. The result is that I believed a dancer should look a certain way, and I've had to untangle that belief over time." Beth ran her hand through her hair, and her fringe flopped back neatly.

"Well, it does sound like you've given the topic a lot of thought."

"How diplomatic of you. I'm probably overthinking this." Beth's mouth twitched at the corners as if she were holding back a laugh.

"I like listening to you. Your whole life has been dancing, and that makes you an expert on the subject."

"I suppose it does." Beth laughed. "Want to go back to bed and discover what else I'm an expert in?"

Liz had been planning to wash the dishes. "I'd like that." This was a much better option; the cleaning up could wait a while.

19

Liz was making a habit of asking her rambling friends to Drag Trivia. Over the past few weeks, she'd basically moved in with Beth. She kept a few clothes there, and Beth had given her a key. Liz had altered her routine so she would stay at Beth's a few nights a week. Their schedules didn't overlap much, but they'd made it work thanks to Liz's ability to work flexible hours. Liz went to her place often enough to water her plants. It'd evolved nicely and Liz was comfortable in the way their shared life was tracking.

"What is going on, Liz?" Gita asked. They'd just won again and Sreesha was up at the bar ordering for everyone with their victory vouchers.

"What do you mean?"

"This is the third time you've invited us here, and you keep casting your view around the room. Who are you looking for?"

"I've met someone."

"Here?" Gita's judgemental expression did nothing for the churn in Liz's gut.

"Yes. Here."

Gita shrugged. "It doesn't seem like your kind of thing."

"If you must know—"

"I must." Gita grinned.

"—we met online. I had no idea about this club until…"

Gita grabbed Liz's forearm and squealed. "This is the friend who you met online and then discovered you were the landlord. You own this club?"

"No. Just the building. The club belongs to Beth."

"Beth. As in Elizabeth? You two are going to be Team Lillibet now?"

"Gita! Why am I friends with you?"

Gita laughed. "Because I tell you what you need to hear. Who noted all the red flags around Petunia? Me."

"Now isn't the time for a 'I told you so', Gita." Liz sighed. "And yes, thank you. I didn't listen to you when you warned me about Petunia. Everyone else only saw the pleasant version of her, and I wanted you to be wrong."

"It's not a failing to see the best in people. Now tell me about this Beth of yours."

Liz's face flushed. "She's nothing like Petunia, for a start. She's abrupt and brave and she's very aware of the power imbalance between us."

Gita raised one eyebrow. "In what way?"

"Settle your feathers, Gita! In the way that she knows her worth and she's not afraid to talk about it. She doesn't cosy up to me or pretend to be something she isn't to gain an advantage. She scraps for everything and makes me earn…"

"Stop."

"Okay?" Liz picked up her empty glass and toyed with it, needing to do something with her hands.

"Start from the beginning. I remember you saying something at dinner ages ago about how you'd messed up a friendship. I want to understand this whole story."

"We talked about this, how she was angry at me for evicting a friend and treating her so callously. Remember at dinner, I said that if I wanted to save the friendship, I'd have to give up my plans and I didn't want to do that…"

"Because of Petunia, yeah. Didn't I give you some useful advice about finding a middle ground?"

"You did. So I bought the buildings next door, and I'm going to demolish them first, and build something new with Beth's club moving into the new building, then I'll demolish this building and do the same again."

"Far out, Liz. Your solution to the problem was just to buy more buildings? I always forget how rich you are, even after the Petunia situation."

Liz shook her head. "Hush, Gita. This time my lawyers have it under control."

"Good. I'd hate for you to go through another mess like that."

"Another mess like what?" Beth slung her arm around Liz's waist and Liz flinched in surprise.

"You must be Beth."

"Yes. Hello."

Liz hauled in a breath. "Beth, this is my friend Gita. Gita, Beth."

"Now Beth, tell me—" Gita's tone held zero sympathy and Liz wanted to sink under the table at the potential awkwardness between Gita and Beth.

"Gita. I don't need you to protect me."

"Maybe you don't need it, but I'm going to do it anyway," Gita said. Beth's arm loosened around Liz's waist, and she wanted to lean against Beth to keep her there.

"What are your intentions with our Liz?" Gita asked. "What guarantees can you give me that you aren't going to take advantage of her?"

Beth laughed as she stepped away from Liz. "Are you kidding me? What guarantee can you give me that Liz isn't going to use her power to destroy my business on a whim?"

"We have a contract and an agreed position." Liz flinched at Beth's harsh response to Gita's taunting.

"And you have a friend who thinks I might take advantage of you. What a lot of shit." Beth folded her arms and glared at Gita. Thankfully, at Gita.

"Liz is more vulnerable than you think."

"Liz is right here and she can speak for herself." Beth said the perfect thing to counter Gita's overprotectiveness.

"You are good, you know that," Gita said.

"What do you mean?"

"Petunia sucked Liz into a toxic relationship with charm. You are doing the same by telling Liz who she is. I don't trust you."

Beth raised one eyebrow but didn't say anything. The silence stretched out awkwardly.

"Well?" Gita asked.

"Like I said, Liz can speak for herself. And frankly, I don't care if you trust me or not. My relationship with Liz isn't your business."

Gita squared her shoulders, and Liz quickly patted her on the hand. She cared for both Beth and Gita and to see them at loggerheads with each other was surprisingly stressful. Liz just wanted her friends to like her lover, and vice versa.

"It's okay, Gita. You don't need to defend me." Liz sighed. "I suppose I have a story to tell, Beth." Liz really didn't want to go into the past and lay out all the ways she'd fallen for a con-artist. Admitting it out loud was a type of defeat in itself.

"You don't need to give her ideas, Liz. Why would you do that?"

"Because Beth isn't Petunia. For years you've told me that I need to get over what Petunia did and start trusting people again, and as soon as I do that, you're all upset about it."

"I just don't want to see you get hurt again, and Beth is all caught up in the business side of your life, just like Petunia was. The parallels are too much. Petunia started out working for you and Beth does too, in a roundabout way."

Liz didn't want Gita to be right, but she didn't want to make the same mistake again. "I'm sorry, Beth."

"For?"

"I think Gita is right." Liz closed her eyes. All through the dramas with Petunia, Gita had been the only one who'd seen the truth. It would be a disaster to ignore Gita again. "I was hoping this would be different because you aren't nice like Petunia, and you have always been honest about what you've wanted from me. But I thought she was honest too, and it turned into a mess. I'm going home now—" Before she fell completely and irreversibly in love with Beth.

Liz couldn't look at Beth because then Beth would know the truth. It was too late. She was already in love and now

Gita had pointed out the parallels between Beth and Petunia and her money and it was all a big mess. One that she'd rather walk away from now before she got screwed over again.

"So much for valuing our friendship, then? Can I count on you to, at least, upload your end of the bargain for my club?" Beth's confirmation that she was just like Petunia and only cared about the money stung like a slap to the face. Liz hoped her disappointment wasn't written all over her face.

"I run my business with integrity."

"As do I, Liz, and yet here we are. You are accusing me of a crime without letting me know what it is and before I've even done anything. I don't care why your friend doesn't like me, but I'm too old to put up with random accusations with no substance. Enjoy your evening. Please come again." Beth walked away with her shoulders square. Liz stared at her, and with every step, her heart sank. She was torn between believing Gita—who'd seen trouble last time—and wanting to run after Beth and apologise.

"I'm sorry, Liz." Gita's apology didn't help.

"For what?"

"This sucks. I don't want to see you go through the same hell again, but you are my friend and this obviously hurts you."

"Last time you were right. That's good enough for me." Liz couldn't trust her judgement on matters of love. Love? Oh boy, this was going to hurt so much. "I'm going home now."

"Hey, Liz. Are you okay? You look like you've seen a ghost." Sreesha arrived with drinks.

"What took you so long?" Gita grabbed her drink off the tray Sreesha was carrying.

"I met an old friend at the bar. I figured you two wouldn't mind. You were chatting to the owner anyway."

"You know Beth?" Liz asked. The twist in her heart when Sreesha mentioned Beth told her everything she needed to know. She was in love, and she'd let Gita—and all her own doubts—make a mess of it.

"No. Les knows everyone though. He's a regular here and introduced me to a few people. Beth apparently runs a tight ship here. Her staff have stuck with her for years. Impressive in hospitality." Sreesha ought to know, he ran the business side of his family's restaurant. "And Les was saying they've got an amazing new chef. I want to come back to dinner sometime."

"Excuse me. I need to use the facilities." With that terrible excuse, Gita jumped up and walked away. Liz rubbed her eyes. Should she chase after Gita? Or just let her be? Beth's voice rang in her head—we aren't bloody teenagers! Relationships should get easier with age, instead, knowing more about life seemed to make it all more complex.

"What happened?"

"Where do I start?"

"Hey. You don't need to say anything. I'll just sit here with you if that's what you need," Sreesha said.

"Thanks." She appreciated the way Sreesha knew when she needed to quietly mull something over. After a while, Liz realised something. "Can I ask you a question?"

"Yes."

"Is it weird being friends with me and having me as your landlady?"

Sreesha shrugged. "No. You've never made it weird. What is this about?"

"I've been seeing Beth—"

"Beth, the owner of Seraph's? Oh…" Sreesha dragged out the sound. "That's why you keep bringing us here for trivia. You own this building?"

"Yes. And I didn't mean to fall in love with her. Shit." Liz pressed the heels of her hands against her eyes until she was certain she wasn't going to cry.

"Hey, it's okay. And to answer your question, no, it's never been weird because you've never made it weird. Like, at first it was a little difficult to let you into my life as a friend because you were this hotshot property investor and I was a … well, a bit of a rascal."

Liz let herself smile a little. "Remember when you said, 'in the 90s you were buying property and I was riding the party tube after midnight with rock stars and people fucked up on coke.' It's amazing that we became friends, we are so different."

"Those were good times!" Sreesha laughed. Liz hadn't known him back then, but she'd heard plenty of his stories while they'd walked the countryside together.

"Do you regret those choices now?"

"Hell no. I'm content to help run the family restaurant." Sreesha's sister was the chef, it was a true family affair. "I suppose I could have spent more time when I was younger on earning enough money to buy the building from you, rather than have the restaurant continue to pay rent all these years, but I'd rather enjoy life than be miserable in the pursuit of money."

"That's where we are different. You tear through life like a whirlwind, and I like to steadily build something over time."

"True. Working for my family is the best job for someone like me. It matters because it's family, but it also allows me to live my life without needing to climb a career ladder or anything stressful like that."

"Do you have no ambitions?" Liz teased and Sreesha laughed as he clicked his glass against hers.

"My ambition is to enjoy life. Do you regret spending so much time working?"

"No. Not at all, not even when Petunia stole all that money from me. I regret trusting her."

Sreesha's mouth dropped open. "Oh, now I understand why you were upset with Gita just now, and why she's run off. Gita is convinced that Beth is another Petunia, and you agreed because Gita was the only one cynical enough to see Petunia for who she was."

"Basically, yes."

"You know that Gita sees the worst in everyone. Why are you letting her influence your choices? She's not always correct."

"But what if she is? It took me years to recover from…" Liz couldn't finish that sentence. "I'm not sure I can do that again."

Sreesha tilted his head and Liz held her breath, awaiting his pronouncement. "The bigger question is … can you live without Beth? Is she worth the risk of history repeating?"

Liz gulped. "I don't know."

"Then walk away, because until you know that she's worth that risk, then she isn't worth it. That's how I knew Matias was the one for me. I was willing to give up everything for him. I didn't have to but being willing to do it was the key to knowing he was the right person for me."

"It's too early to know," Liz lied. From the moment Sreesha had asked if Beth was worth the risk, she'd known what she wanted. Was she brave enough to try?

20

————

Beth had had better nights. First the weird argument with Liz, and then being confronted by her friend afterwards. It was all far too much drama for a friends with benefits situation, although it did point favourably towards this emerging relationship mattering more to Liz than just whatever they were doing at the moment.

Beth couldn't let herself hope. She had only just figured out that she was ready for a new relationship, ready to allow someone into her life and her heart, when it had suddenly turned messy. She was too independent to bother with mess like this.

"Are you coming down with something?" Charlie pressed her palm against Beth's forehead.

"No."

"You look terrible."

"Thanks a lot."

"I'm serious. Are you sure you aren't sick?" Charlie was the only one of the Seraph's staff who'd had COVID, and she'd gone from careless about her health to seeing illness everywhere.

"I'm fine. Just tired." Ever since Gita had confronted her, Beth hadn't been able to stop thinking about what bullshit her concern was. Liz knew they were doing friends with benefits for one simple reason: Liz always kept her distance. They only ever slept at Beth's flat, most likely because it was conveniently located upstairs, yet Beth occasionally wondered what Liz's place was like. It might be nice to be invited to see it some-time. Liz would drop by, hang out at the bar for a while, then head upstairs, and when Beth was finished for the night, she'd go home and sleep. They'd gotten into the habit of having sex in the mornings after Beth had had a decent sleep. It was lovely, except for the fact that Liz kept Beth at arms-length.

"I can lock up tonight if you need to get some rest."

"No. You go home to Elle." Beth would go home to her empty flat and lie awake reliving tonight's conversations. It made no sense for Gita to be so concerned for Liz. The power imbalance between them favoured Liz. If anyone should be worried, it was Beth. The fucking audacity of her friend to assume Beth would take advantage of Liz was stag-gering. How was that even possible?

"Only if you promise to rest properly. I don't want to see you here tomorrow night if you still look so poorly."

Beth sucked in a tight breath between her teeth. "I'm the boss, Charlie. I'll decide on my schedule."

"Hey, you are allowed to let other people care for you. You don't have to be the one who cares about us all the time."

"Fine. I will try to rest. You and Walter can lock up."

Beth bolted to her unit, feeling every one of the stairs in her stump. Why was she even upset about not having seen Liz's house? It shouldn't matter because she wasn't going to let herself fall in love with Liz anyway. Her skin prickled—too fucking late for that. She'd already fallen for Liz and she wanted everything. The fucking mean-spirited irony in realising that just as Liz's friend poisoned her thoughts to think the worst of Beth was an added punch in the guts.

She walked inside and flopped onto her only chair, took off her leg, and massaged her stump.

"Would you like some water?"

Beth screamed. "Fucking hell." Her heart went a million miles an hour. "What the fuck are you doing here?"

"Sorry. Did I scare you?"

"Yeah." Beth pressed her hand against her breastbone to try and keep her heart inside her chest. Holy shit. "Why are you here?"

"I think we should talk."

Beth held up one hand. "Give me a moment. And fuck it, pour me a bourbon too."

"Okay. I'm sorry. I thought you'd seen me." Liz walked into the kitchen and poured Beth a good sized slosh of bourbon into a glass. "Here you are."

"Thanks." Beth gulped at it, letting the fiery alcoholic burn in her throat help settle down her racing pulse.

"I'm very confused. Gita thinks I shouldn't trust you and Sreesha thinks I should."

"Don't you have any thoughts of your own?"

From the way, Liz's eyes widened, Beth knew she'd been a bit harsh, but damn it, she was still recovering from having Liz appear out of nowhere in her house.

"Um, I do, but I don't trust them. My thoughts, I mean."

Beth rolled her eyes. "Spare me the bloody sob story. This evening your friend accused me of some fucking thing, I don't even know what. And to add insult to injury, she didn't just do it in front of you, but chased me across my place of business to have a second crack at me."

"Really? I'm sorry. Gita is a little overprotective of me."

"Why is that?" Beth was curious. She'd been content to keep Liz as a friend with benefits and not think too hard about why she'd never been invited to her house. The one-sided-ness of this—whatever it was—was going to annoy Beth at some point. Like right now.

"A long time ago, I…" Liz paused. "I'm sorry, this is really hard for me to talk about."

"But not so hard for Gita to think I'll repeat whatever it is. If I'm going to be judged, at least let me know the details of that judgement."

"That's fair." Liz paced back and forth across the room. "I've avoided talking about this for so long I don't know where to start."

"And you are still avoiding it." Beth just wanted to go to bed and pretend she'd never let herself get involved with this messy drama. She was too old and too busy and too fucking tired for all of this.

"I got scammed. There, I said it. I'm embarrassed about it and I hate talking about it."

"Oh no. Are you okay?" Beth hadn't expected that. Not the revelation, or the way Liz was so obviously uncomfortable in admitting she was the victim of fraud.

"It was a long time ago. Petunia worked for me, and we

slowly fell in love. Or so I thought. I was about to propose to her when she disappeared with nearly a million pounds."

"Like gone?"

"Yes. She stole from me and…"

"The police?" Beth hadn't expected that story. She knew asking about the police was probably pointless, but she had to say something.

"Have never found her. She used a fake name. For four years, she worked for me and then lived with me. It was all a long con and I'm embarrassed that I fell for it."

"Wow. That sounds really traumatic." Beth wanted to reach out and hug Liz and reassure her that it wasn't her fault. Beth would never do that to her.

Oh fuck.

A nasty prickle of fury gathered at the base of her spine, growing like a vine of thorns wrapping around her body.

"Your friend Gita thought I was going to steal from you too. How dare she. How fucking dare she?" To Beth's surprise, Liz smiled, then lent down and gave her a huge hug.

"Thank you."

"For?"

"For being perfectly you. I doubted myself because I'd let Petunia into my life and here I was again, letting in someone who I already had a financial arrangement with. The parallels were confusing and when Gita showed the same concern, I believed her."

"Okay?" Beth was confused—caught between anger and empathy. "Why believe her?"

"Gita was the only one who noticed something wrong with Petunia's behaviour. She worried that I was changing myself for Petunia, and when Petunia left… Well, hindsight is a great thing, I suppose. I guess I listened to her because she'd been right the last time."

"Makes sense." Beth hated being thrown in the same cynical bucket as a con artist, but at least Liz had a friend looking out for her wellbeing. "This is so ironic."

"Why?" Liz's mouth hung open. "What do you mean?"

"When this all started, I was bothered by the financial power you held over me, and now I find that this whole time you were worried that I'd… Well, anyway. Is that why you refused to negotiate on evicting me?"

"Yes. One of the things I did around Petunia was constantly give in to her demands. If she wanted something, I'd put aside my own plans to give her what she wanted. You have to understand, she was very—"

"Beautiful?"

"No, I mean, she was quite pretty but not conventionally beautiful. Her smile was warm, and her chatter was very charming. She was always happy and pleasant and made me feel like I was the only person in the room who mattered to her."

Beth scoffed. "She stroked your ego."

"Yes. And I fell for it. Big time."

Beth reached out for Liz's hands. "I understand now. Thank you for sharing your story with me and I can see why this was so hard for you to talk about." Beth understood Liz's initial resistance to changing her plans so she didn't have to evict a friend, and why Liz felt she needed to evict her in the first place. She understood why Gita was so protective over Liz, and even why Liz hadn't ever invited Beth home. It couldn't be easy to try and trust someone after such a brutal scheme. To think of Liz conned into love by this Petunia bitch who only used her for money... It broke Beth's heart to see the anguish on Liz's face.

"You do?"

"Of course. You are this big shot property investor, brought down by a pretty face."

"What?"

Beth cringed. Crap. "That didn't come out right. I just meant that if I was a successful business person and I'd been conned, I'd be embarrassed too. I guess I was trying to make a joke."

"How can you joke about this? I let Gita think you would be the same."

"It's either joke or hunt down this Petunia character and punch her in the nose." Beth's instinct was to defend Liz, because if she thought about it too much, the lack of trust Liz had in Beth would remind her to be furious. She'd rather be mad at the vacant Petunia, than at Liz or herself.

"Thank you."

"Don't be thanking me. Look, it's been a long night. I'm going to have a shower and go to sleep. Let's talk more in the morning."

"You want me to stay?"

"Sure, why not?"

"Well, I let my friend think you were going to scam me and break my heart."

Beth scoffed. "It's not your fault that your friend is cyni-cal. Hell, she only said what I would've said if the roles were reversed. Now I know the story, I definitely would have painted myself as a gold digger waiting to empty your accounts. Now get up and let me get up too."

Liz passed Beth her crutches. "Thanks. I think?" The easy way Liz helped her only served to remind Beth of Liz's concerns that Beth would take advantage and she had the nasty urge to … do something unsavoury. How fucking dare Liz's friend think Beth might hurt Liz like this Petunia character had? And fuck—what an odd fake name to pick. Whatever. Beth wasn't going to spend her precious sleeping hours overthinking a past that she had nothing to do with. All of this mess would look clearer in the morning.

L iz stared at Beth's sleeping body and tried to push away the envy at the sight. She hadn't slept at all, and at about six this morning, she'd given up trying and started scrolling on her phone. Most of what she saw was nonsense, but for the last ten minutes, she'd been staring at an inspirational post that said, "People are at their most honest when they don't get what they want." She'd stared so long that her phone had turned off, she'd opened it up again, and it'd turned off again. One simple social media post from someone trying to be philosophical for likes had helped her realise the core difference between Beth and Petunia. There was probably no joy in comparing them, yet she'd fallen for Beth because she reacted to a problem by digging in and working harder. Petunia had always avoided work; using her charm and smile to slide around a task until Liz just did it herself. She should never have let Petunia flirt with her, and she definitely shouldn't have let her boundaries disappear around her until there was nothing of herself left.

"Damn it Liz. I can hear you thinking." Beth rolled over and squinted at her.

"What?"

"Did you sleep at all?"

"Not really. I can't help thinking about the past and how I just let myself disappear. I gave myself away, and ultimately I let Petunia steal from me."

Beth sat up and glared at Liz. "No. You tell that thought to fuck right off. Now. It's not your fault. Her actions are not your fault." Beth's fierce tone almost made Liz believe it was true.

"Seriously, Liz. If you've been blaming yourself for years, then no wonder a few comments from Gita had you second guessing yourself."

"I thought you'd be angry at me."

"Maybe I am, a little bit." Beth's nostrils flared. "But I'm much more angry at her. No one forced Petunia to steal from you. That was her choice, her decision."

"It's so embarrassing though."

Beth nodded. "Yeah, I bet it is. The rich property investor who can make business deals and read contracts and all that stuff gets taken for a ride. Yeah, that's pretty embarrassing."

"Why would you say that?"

"What? You'd rather I bolster your ego?" Beth breathed in slowly. "It's okay to be embarrassed in this situation. It's not okay to blame yourself for someone else's shitty actions." She'd taken the nasty edge off her voice, delivering her advice with a gentle tone.

Liz let out a shaky breath. "One day, you and Gita are going to be best friends and you'll take over the world. In fact, no. That sounds scary. I'm just going to keep the two of you away from each other."

"I don't want to take over the world. I just want my club. I have enough in my life."

"Are you just saying that?"

Beth growled. "No. I'm not just saying that. If you can't trust me, you shouldn't be in my bloody bed."

Liz flinched. "I'm sorry."

"Damn it." Beth rolled on top of Liz and kissed her. "Don't be sorry. Trust is earned and you've had yours trampled. I'm just pissed that I've been tarred with the same brush. Not by you. I need a little time to let my reactions settle."

"I get it. All of this happened a long time ago. I shouldn't let it get to me like this."

Beth kissed her again, a kiss that soothed and apologised and took away some of the anxiety dancing a jig in her skull.

"Time doesn't seem to care about whether something happened yesterday or decades ago. I'm still mad at Jewel for trying to stop me create Seraph's and I still miss her every day. It's okay to have complicated feelings about something. I tell myself Jewel would be proud of me without knowing if it is true, and I've learned to have some peace with that."

"I wish I was so wise."

Beth kissed her, a gentle peck on the lips this time. "You are wise. You listened to your friend's concerns. You took your time to process whether you were repeating old mistakes. You didn't just ignore your instincts."

"My instincts are bad. I love you and I wish I didn't."

"What?" Beth blinked and Liz wished she wasn't stuck underneath her body.

"I mean… I don't know what I mean. I'm so confused. I thought I loved Petunia too."

"Maybe you did. Loving someone doesn't mean they won't hurt you. Love isn't always wise. It doesn't protect you from harm."

"But what does it say about me that I loved her and she did that?"

Beth leaned closer and pressed her cheek against Liz's. "It means that she didn't love you back. It means you wanted her to be someone she wasn't."

"Do you mean that I loved the idea of her?"

"I don't know. Maybe you loved who she said she was. It's not bad to trust someone, and it's their fault if they destroy that trust. Not yours."

"But what if I love you and—"

"And what?"

"And it doesn't work out." Liz knew Beth wouldn't steal from her. It wasn't possible, not with the boundaries and protections her lawyers had put in place since the Petunia incident.

"Is it worth the risk?" Beth asked.

Liz cupped Beth's cheeks. "Have you been talking to Sreesha?"

"Who?"

"One of my other friends. He asked me the same thing. I'd know if it was really love if I was ready to take the risk of being hurt again."

"And?"

"Beth. I love you. I'm pretty confused about a lot of things right now, but I'm sure about that."

Beth answered with a kiss. A proper kiss that tasted like

home, like sunshine after rain, like the pot at the end of the rainbow. And Liz knew that she would take the risk on Beth. From the very start of their online friendship, Beth had always been the same. Abrupt and yet empathetic. She knew who she was and what she wanted, and she had so much passion for her work and her business. Liz could imagine a life together.

"I thought we were just friends with benefits." Beth lifted her head. "Imagine my surprise when all my feelings got involved. I love you, Liz, and you can take as much time as you need. On one condition."

Liz closed her eyes. "No. No conditions." She opened her eyes to see Beth's grin. Beth's eyes glowed with amusement.

"I shouldn't tease you like that. I'm sorry. It's just so tempting, because you get all serious and stern and it's hot."

"It is?" Liz felt like she'd been running down hill and her body was going faster than her legs. Soon she'd fall in a messy heap of tangled limbs.

"It is. And hey, no conditions unless you want them. I'm happy with our current arrangement."

"You are."

"Yes. We can move this along at your pace, when you are comfortable."

"Thank you. I appreciate that." It was why Liz was in love with Beth, because for all her bluster, she was always willing to let Liz make her own decisions. Liz never felt pushed into a corner when she was around Beth.

"It's for my benefit too."

"How so?"

"You have no idea, do you?"

"About?"

"About how fucking attractive you are when you are certain about something. That first meeting we had, when you granted me ten minutes to state my case, and then you said, 'Nope, my plans are all that matter'. I was so mad at you, but also so turned on. So wet for you."

Liz's face burned bright hot. "Really?"

"Yes. Be certain. Be yourself. Even when it's going to make me mad. I don't want you to hide yourself from me. I don't want you to change your plans for me. I'll fight them when they are wrong, but don't change for my sake. I like it. No, scratch that. I love it when you are certain."

Liz knew there was only one option. She rolled them both so she lay on top of Beth and she kissed her with the certainty that this was love. An imperfect love between two determined independent people, but perhaps that's why it would last. This was the kiss of champions, the one that said all the things she was certain of in her heart. The kiss that took all the risks on love and poured them directly from her heart into Beth's heart. She wanted to do this, to take a chance on Beth, no matter the risks ahead.

21

Six weeks later, Beth grinned as she sat on the edge of the stage, her legs dangling over the side. Life didn't get any better than this. All the staff at Seraph's were gathered around, staring at her. Well, she'd asked them here to have a chat before Liz's fiftieth birthday party tonight.

"Let's run through the program for tonight." Everyone groaned. Fair enough too, because if she was honest with herself, she'd planned this party far beyond what it needed and bugged everyone about all the annoying details until they were all bored with talking about it. Over the last six weeks, they'd embedded the new schedule and it was going better than Beth had hoped. All the staff were enjoying the extra night off—on the weeks they weren't fully booked out for office Christmas parties—and the other nights had been making enough of a profit that she was able to make this announcement now. "But before that, there's one thing I'd like to announce."

The switch from boredom to interest on everyone's faces was hilarious. She couldn't wait to tell Liz about it.

"Come on. Don't leave us all hanging!" Yolande called out and everyone laughed.

"Okay. Since we reopened, London has really embraced going out and we've done well. I've done the figures and…" Beth paused for dramatic effect, and when everyone jeered, she grinned. "Everyone gets a ten percent rise, effective immediately."

"Woah, seriously?" Charlie was the first to answer. Most people just stood there gaping at her.

"Yes, I'm serious. I have formal letters for everyone. I'll email them to everyone tonight, have a read through, and sign if you are happy."

"Thank you. I reckon I speak for everyone when I say that's totally cool." Charlie said.

"Okay. Let's talk about tonight, and then we can get to work. And hey, everyone…" The pause made the potential for a laugh even better. "Don't spend it all at once." Beth grinned as they all laughed. "Okay, okay. Tonight is pretty simple. We are closed for a birthday party. We aren't doing any burlesque, so we can set up a display on the front of the stage. Elle, you've got that under control?"

"Yes."

"Honestly, Beth. We know it's your girlfriend's party and everything, but we've been over these details twenty times this week. It's going to be fine." Charlie said.

"Let's be certain about that." She tried to sound nonchalant, but given the way everyone grinned back at her, she knew she'd missed the mark. It was hardly the first private party they'd held here, so Beth didn't need to stress quite this much. Her team knew what they were doing.

"It's going to be fine. We have two hours until people

arrive. Let's go." Charlie's certainty sent everyone scooting away to do the tasks they'd decided on a few weeks ago. "I'm right, you know. You are stressing far too much because it's Liz's party." Charlie patted Beth on the knee. "We've got this."

"You're just saying that because I gave you a pay rise." Beth slid off the stage. It was easier to chat to Charlie without being weirdly above her.

"It's okay to be nervous. We are going to put on the best party imaginable for the love of your life."

"Get out of here." Beth laughed as Charlie spoke the truth. "Why don't you go and help Elle with that giant flower arrangement?"

"Okay." Charlie gave Beth a quick hug and paced off to give Elle and Ben a hand. The flower arrangement consisted of fifty pot plants—one for each year—that Liz could add to her collection. Beth had gone through the old forums and put together a list of all the plants Liz had mentioned over the years, all her favourites and all the ones she wanted to have one day.

~

The party was a huge success. Beth took a moment to soak in the atmosphere. She closed her eyes and breathed in deep. The smells of people's sweat as they danced, and beer splashed on the floor, and all the usual scents of a warm room filled with drunk people filled her nostrils and she adored it. All their energy literally filled her with joy. But not as much as seeing her Liz laughing with all her friends. That amazing woman, who had built her business again after such a financially and emotionally devastating moment, was in love with Beth. Beth couldn't believe her luck. She thought she'd had her one true love. To find another was the stuff of legends.

"Why aren't you dancing? Is your leg sore?" Liz asked.

"No, it's fine. I was enjoying watching you dance."

"Is it time for the speeches yet?"

Beth held Liz's hands. "Whenever you are ready."

"Oh, I'm ready. I've never been more ready for anything in my life."

"I'd better get you the microphone then." Beth walked up the steps at the edge of the stage and turned off the music. "Hello everyone. Thank you for attending Liz's fiftieth birthday party. The birthday girl wants to say a few words." She handed over the microphone to Liz, who strode onto the middle of the stage with all the confidence of one of Beth's dancers. Maybe one day… No, that was a thought for another day.

"Thank you everyone for coming to my party. And especially to Gita who organised all of this." Liz paused while everyone clapped. She was a natural on stage. If Beth hadn't spent the last week coaching her and helping her rehearse her speech, she would've believed Liz did this all the time.

"The thing about being fifty is that I'm set in my ways. I love a good ramble. I'm thankful for all my friends. And you all know how much I love my plants. This present is the absolute best present ever. Thank you for each plant, they'll all get so much love and attention." Liz paused as everyone applauded. "The funny thing about being fifty is that it marks the age when I definitely have less years left to live than I've already enjoyed. Even if I'm lucky enough to make it to one hundred, I'm already halfway, and that adds a sense of urgency to everything. I don't want to wait any more. It would be so easy to have a simple relationship with Beth where we enjoy each other's company without pressing the issue…"

Beth swallowed. This wasn't in the speech that Liz had rehearsed with her.

"I am completely and utterly head over heels in love with Beth." The crowd roared with cheers of approval. "When she's ready, I'd like to marry her. You'll all be invited to the wedding." Liz put the microphone back in its stand, walked over to Beth, and kissed her. The uproar of noise surrounded Beth until the beauty of Liz's kiss made everything melt away.

Liz had overcome her doubts and announced her love in front of all her friends. Beth wanted to swoon. She let herself be swept away in the kiss and it wasn't until Liz lifted her face that she noticed the crowd had stopped cheering. Everyone stared expectedly. Beth bowed to the crowd, then grabbed the microphone, turning to Liz and pretending to ignore everyone. She loved this type of showmanship, couldn't resist performing for people, and hopefully Liz wouldn't mind the suspense either.

"Isn't it obvious? Yes. I'll marry you, Liz. Whenever you are ready."

"Good. Now let's party." Charlie's voice rang out above the crowd. Beth grabbed Liz's hand and marched across the stage. She turned on the music and pulled Liz backstage for another kiss.

"I can't believe you said yes."

"I can't believe you asked me."

"It's real, Beth. I love you."

"Let's do it. But I want a prenup." Beth needed to let Liz know that she wasn't going to do anything awful.

"You don't need that." Liz's trust was beautiful and Beth wanted to adorn herself in it.

"No. But you do." Beth emphasised the 'you' deliberately so Liz couldn't misinterpret her point. "I want you to be protected, no matter what happens in the future. Trust me on this one."

"I do trust you."

"I know. That's why we will sign a prenup agreement. This matters to you and therefore it matters to me." Beth didn't want Liz to ever have doubts about her choice, and she was perfectly content with her club. She didn't need access to Liz's money. She only needed Liz to go forward with all the protections she needed to stop the past rearing its ugly head between them again. "Trust me on this one. If we sign this agreement, it removes all doubt and it's one thing we never have to fight about."

"One thing?"

"Oh, I'm going to fight with you about all sorts of things. I want this one taken off the table."

Liz smiled. "You are the best."

"I know." Beth winked just before she pulled Liz closer for a long decadent kiss. "I love you and I want to see you thrive."

"Good. I have one condition too." Liz paused.

"Which is?"

"You need to come on holiday with me. One week now, and at least two weeks every six months."

"Agreed." Beth had spent years skirting with burnout,

being the only one responsible for the club. The idea of a holiday—and letting her highly competent staff run the place for a while without her—sounded scary. And incredible. She knew the reason why. Because Liz would be with her. "You won't mind if I sleep for most of that time?"

"No. We can go somewhere remote. I'll walk outside, and you can sleep inside. It sounds perfect."

"Perfect, huh?"

"Yes."

"I know one thing that will guarantee perfection." Beth winked. "Come up to my bed and I'll show you."

"Now?"

"Yes. No one will miss us. We can come back to your party later."

"Okay. Take me to your bed, Beth. Let me demonstrate how much I love you."

Want a bit more sexy romance and see how Liz and Beth are getting on? Read the exclusive epilogue and the grand opening of Seraph's Burlesque Club in the new building when you sign up for my newsletter. The Seraph's Burlesque Club series begins with SHOW UP.

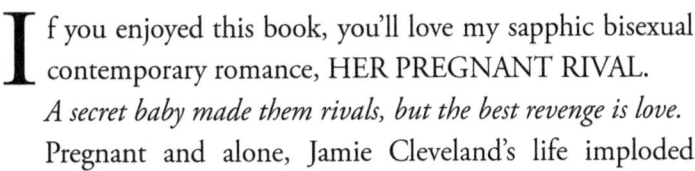

If you enjoyed this book, you'll love my sapphic bisexual contemporary romance, HER PREGNANT RIVAL.

A secret baby made them rivals, but the best revenge is love.

Pregnant and alone, Jamie Cleveland's life imploded

when her lover revealed he was married. The cheating is bad enough, but if Jamie's controlling father discovers she's about to be a single mom, he'll pull her trust fund. Jamie's fashion blogging is glamorous, but doesn't pay. Worse still, if she goes it alone, her mother might pay the price for her disobedience, and Jamie can't allow that. So it's just Jamie's luck that when she walks into a prenatal appointment and finds the wife of her baby's father is her doctor.

Knowing your soon to be ex-husband is a cheating pig is one thing, but being confronted by the gorgeous woman he's been sleeping with is quite another. Especially since she's pregnant, desperate, and clearly alone, when she most needs family. Dr Amanda Aitken knows she ought to hate Jamie, but all she can feel is compassion. . . and a frisson of attraction.

On a whim, Amanda invites Jamie to get to know her child's half-siblings, and brings her enemy irresistibly close. They can't fight their desire, but when the men in their lives find out, they'll have a war between duty and love. . .

Society expects them to be rivals, and neither of them expect that the best revenge is to love each other.

AUTHOR NOTES

The Ramblers (ramblers.org.uk) is a UK charity that maintains and protects walking paths around the country. The UK has a network of publicly available pathways across the countryside that are open for anyone to use and these are supported by various Acts of Parliament such as the Countryside and Rights of Way Act.

There is a wonderful show created by the Australian Broadcasting Corporation called "You can't ask that." They did an episode on amputees and here are two great quotes from it:

"It's never comfortable. I've just learned to be uncomfortable." Glenn Dickson Qld.

"Do you wear your leg when you are having sex?" "Do you wear your shoes? It's the same thing." – Peter Stringer Adelaide.

ACKNOWLEDGMENTS

I pay my respects to the Wangal people of the Eora Nation, who are the traditional owners of the land on which this book was written.

Thank you to my beta readers, Terry Mehlman, Renee Bartray, Anne-Benedicte Damon, who untangled the conflicts and plot issues I was having and hopefully made this into a satisfying romance. Thanks also to my editor, Lauriel Masson-Oakden of LMO Editing, who edited this whole series and tried her best to keep my grammar consistent. The covers were done by Sarah Paige, who has done many of my covers, and has a wonderful eye for design.

As always, thanks need to go to Ali, Torrance, Marie, and Kait who helped hold me together while I was writing and editing this series. There is a long backstory behind the publication of this series that was often incredibly stressful as rights were untangled and corrected. I couldn't have made it through all of that without our DMs reminding me that this series was worth the stress.

ALL BOOKS BY RENÉE DAHLIA

Thanks for reading SHOW QUEEN. I hope you enjoyed it. Reviews can help readers find books, and I am grateful for all honest reviews. Thank you for taking the time to let others know what you've read, and what you thought. If you write a review for SHOW QUEEN and email me with the link, I will send you a free copy of any of my other books of your choice. My email is renee at reneedahlia dot com.

If you'd like to know more about me, my books, or to connect with me online, you can visit my webpage www.reneedahlia.com and if you sign up to my newsletter, you can grab a free book.

Twitter
https://twitter.com/dekabat
Facebook
https://www.facebook.com/reneedahliawriter/
Instagram
https://www.instagram.com/reneedahlia_author/

You've just read a book in my Seraph's Burlesque Club Series.

Contemporary Series: Seraph's Burlesque Club

1. Show Up (ff with bisexual heroine)
2. Show Off (ff with bisexual heroines)
3. Show Queen (ff)
4. TBA Duo of Novellas (mm)

Contemporary Series: Kapow!

1. Out of Her League (fm with bisexual characters)
2. His Buxom Beauty (fm)
3. Craving His Spotlight (mm)
4. Her Pregnant Rival (ff)

Contemporary Series: Farrellton Foster Family

1. Betrayed (fm)
2. Forbidden (fm with bisexual characters)
3. Liability (ff)

Contemporary Series: Margaret River TV: Boxed Set

- Homage (fm with bisexual heroine)
- Uplift (ff with bisexual heroines)

Contemporary Series: Merindah Park

1. Merindah Park (fm)
2. Making Her Mark (fm with bisexual heroine)

3. <u>Two Hearts Healing (fm)</u>
4. <u>Racetrack Royalty (fm)</u>

Contemporary Series: Rainbow Cove

1. <u>His Christmas Pearl (fm)</u>
2. His Christmas Pride (mm)

Historical Series: Great War

1. Her Lady's Melody (ff)
2. Her Lady's Fortune (ff)
3. <u>Her Lady's Honor (ff)</u>
4. His Lord's Soldier (mm)

Historical Series: Bluestockings

Prequel: The Shipwrecked Earl's Bride (fm with bisexual hero)

1. <u>To Charm a Bluestocking (fm with bisexual hero)</u>
2. <u>In Pursuit of a Bluestocking (fm)</u>
3. <u>The Heart of a Bluestocking (fm)</u>